Nouveau
Cahier du jour
Cahier du soir

4e

13-14 ans

Anglais LV1

W0402253

Auteurs

Nicole de Vannoise
Jean Cureau
Professeurs d'Anglais au collège

Auteur du mémento

Coline Segonne
Professeur d'Anglais au collège

MAGNARD

Présentation

Un cahier complet

- **Ce cahier d'Anglais, destiné aux élèves de 4e, est conforme aux derniers programmes.** Il reprend toutes les notions et couvre tous les domaines.
- **La rubrique « Observer et retenir »** propose toutes les **leçons** accompagnées d'**exemples**.
- **La rubrique « S'entraîner »** propose des **exercices progressifs** pour réinvestir les acquisitions. Ils sont classés par niveau de difficulté (de ★ à ★★★).
- À la fin de chaque page, l'élève est invité à **s'auto-évaluer**.

→ *Les corrigés détachables sont situés au centre du cahier.*

Un mémento visuel

Un mémento avec l'essentiel à retenir en Anglais 4e :
pour une mémorisation visuelle efficace !

→ *À détacher au centre du cahier et à conserver toute l'année.*

POUR LE CAHIER :
Illustration de couverture : Auren – **Illustrations intérieures :** Pénélope Paicheler – **Conception graphique (couverture) :** Yannick Le Bourg et Raphaël Hadid – **Mise en pages :** Facompo – **Cartographie :** Valérie Goncalves, Marie-Christine Liennard, Christel Parolini

POUR LE MÉMENTO VISUEL DÉTACHABLE :
Illustrations : Aurélie Verdon – **Mise en pages :** Linéale

© Éditions Magnard, 2019, Paris.
www.joursoir.fr

Aux termes du Code de la propriété intellectuelle, toute reproduction ou représentation intégrale ou partielle de la présente publication, faite par quelque procédé que ce soit (reprographie, microfilmage, scannérisation, numérisation...) sans le consentement de l'auteur ou de ses ayants droit ou ayants cause est illicite et constitue une contrefaçon sanctionnée par les articles L. 335-2 et suivants du Code de la propriété intellectuelle.
L'autorisation d'effectuer des reproductions par reprographie doit être obtenue auprès du Centre Français d'exploitation du droit de la Copie (CFC) 20, rue des Grands-Augustins – 75006 PARIS – Tél. : 01 44 07 47 70 – Fax : 01 46 34 67 19

DANGER LE PHOTOCOPILLAGE TUE LE LIVRE

Sommaire

VOCABULAIRE ET CIVILISATION

GRAMMAIRE

ANNEXES

Mémento visuel détachable

Corrigés détachables au centre du cahier

1 Le sport et la santé
Sport and health

→ Corrigés p. I

Observer et retenir

Let's keep fit!

The football ground

1. a soccer player
2. a crowd (a lot of supporters)
3. the referee
4. the goal
5. the goalkeeper
6. the scoreboard
7. the coach

Body care, cosmetics

makeup

perfume

shampoo

soap

a brush

earrings

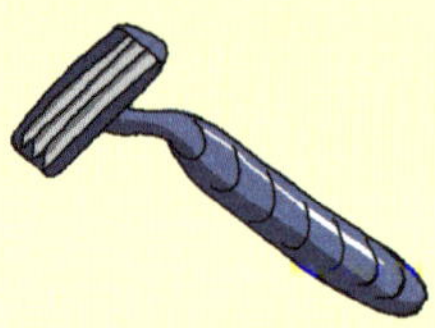
a razor (shaver)

a handbag

a handkerchief
a hanky

a purse

Health vs. illness

The doctor comes

PATIENT: Good morning, doctor. I feel really **sick** and **weak**. All my **limbs** are **painful**. It's very **tiring**. I'm **tired**.

DOCTOR: I see. You've got **a headache**. You **have a temperature**. You must have caught **a cold**.

PATIENT: Is it a serious **disease**?

DOCTOR: Not really. You must have got **the flu**. I'll give you some **medicines**. What you need is some **rest**.

PATIENT: Thank you, doctor. You are saving my life!

S'entraîner

1 ★ Complétez les phrases avec les mots indiqués ci-dessous afin de leur donner un sens.

attend (verbe) – *coach* (nom) – *goal* (n.) – *score* (v.) – *scoreboard* (n.) – *seat* (n.) – *support* (v.) – *team* (n.) – *train* (v.) – *versus* ou *vs.* (préposition)

1. Today there is a great match. Aston Villa ....VS..... Arsenal.
2. Aston Villa and Arsenal are two very good teams
3. So there are a lot of supporters to attend the match; there is not one ....seat.... left.
4. But the ....coach.... of Aston Villa has ....trained.... his team particularly well.
5. Look at the ....scoreboard....! Aston Villa has ....scored.... 3 ....goals.....
6. All those that ....supporters.... Aston Villa are enthusiastic.

2 ★★ Répondez aux questions suivantes.

1. What do you use when your hair is dirty?
When my hair is dirty I use shampoo
2. What do men use in the morning?
In the morning men use a shaver
3. What do you need to wash?
I need soap to wash
4. What do ladies put their purses in?
Ladies put coins in their purse
5. What do people use when they have a cold?
The people use tissues when they have cold.
6. What do girls put on when they go to a party?
Girls put on makeup when they go to a party.
7. What smells so good here?
Perfume smells so good here
8. What do ladies put on their faces to look elegant?
....
9. Where do you put your money in?
....
10. What do you use to tidy your hair in the morning?
....

3 ★★ Complétez les phrases suivantes en utilisant des mots du dialogue de la page 4.

1. Here's a thermometer. You must take your ....temperature....
2. I've got a headache....... Give me some aspirin and a glass of water.
3. I've just caught a cold. Don't worry! It isn't a serious ....disease........
4. What's on the prescription? – Just a few ....medicines.....
5. You look tired. Stop working and have a ....rest.................

4 ★★★ Reliez par une flèche les deux parties de chaque phrase suivant le sens.

1. She was ill •		• a. she couldn't find a seat in the stadium.
2. There were too many supporters •		• b. she bought handkerchiefs.
3. She trained the players very well •	so	• c. her team won.
4. She had a cold •		• d. she had to stay at home.
5. The goalkeeper was very good •		• e. she was elected "coach of the year".

Auto évaluation Très bien ☐ Bien ☐ Pas assez bien ☐

2 La nourriture, le restaurant
Food, the restaurant

→ Corrigés p. I

Observer et retenir

Animals → Meat

ox (or cow) → beef

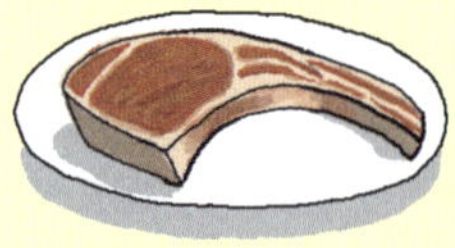

sheep → mutton

calf → veal

pig → pork

turkey → turkey

Vegetables

1. mushrooms
2. french beans
3. peas
4. cauliflower
5. potatoes

Fruit, dessert

1. pineapple
2. lemon
3. strawberries
4. pudding
5. grapes
6. cottage cheese

Drinks

1. beer
2. wine
3. milk
4. water
5. coffee
6. white coffee

A dialogue at the end of the meal

CUSTOMER: Waiter, the **bill**, please.

WAITER: Here you are. Pay at the **counter**, please.

CASHIER: £20. Do you pay **cash** or by cheque?

CUSTOMER: I've got my credit card… But let me **check** the bill first… It's all right. Well, I think I'll pay cash.

CASHIER: Your **change**, sir.

CUSTOMER: Thank you… Here's the **tip** for the **waiter**. Goodbye.

S'entraîner

1 ★ Trouvez les deux mots qui sont cachés dans chaque suite de lettres.

1. BBEEEEFR

→ .... → ....

2. CEEFFIKLMO

→ .... → ....

3. HMMMNOOORSTTUU

→ .... → ....

4. AABEEFGIPRRRRRSTTUWY

→ .... → ....

2 ★ À l'aide des définitions, retrouvez l'ordre des lettres pour former les mots.

1. It swims in the water.

FHIS → ....

2. The English's favourite drink

AET → ....

3. A yellow fruit

AAABNN → ....

4. An orange vegetable

TRACRO → ....

5. Eaten at tea-time

BCIISSTU → ....

6. Out of which wine is served

BELOTT → ....

7. Red fruit eaten in June

CEHRRY → ....

8. Grilled bread for breakfast

AOSTT → ....

9. What you order in a fast-food restaurant

ABEGHMRRU → ....

10. What I can cut my meat with

EFIKN → ....

3 ★★ Mettez les mots dans l'ordre pour faire des phrases utiles au restaurant.

1. bring – could – me – menu – the – you – ?

→ ....

2. have – I'd – like – some – to – water – .

→ ....

3. do – have – salad – tomato – you – ?

→ ....

4. bill – can – have – I – please – the – ?

→ ....

5. included – is – the – tip – ?

→ ....

4 ★★★ Vous allez dans un restaurant végétarien. Imaginez le menu.

Menu

....

....

....

....

....

....

....

5 ★★★ Que suis-je ?

1. I am yellow and bitter.

....

2. I grow in the woods.

....

3. I am a chip. What am I made from?

....

4. I am perfectly transparent.

....

Auto évaluation Très bien ☐ Bien ☐ Pas assez bien ☐

3 La vie et le travail
Life and work

→ Corrigés p. I

Observer et retenir

Life

a kid

a teenager

a grown-up

an old woman

Nouns	**Verbs**
birth	be born
engagement	get engaged to someone
marriage	get married to someone / marry someone
divorce	get divorced from someone / divorce someone
death	die

Trades

artist

cashier

clerk

cook

detective

engineer

manager

mechanic

nurse

receptionist

sailor

scientist

shop assistant

traffic warden

waiter (m.) / waitress (f.)

S'entraîner

1 ★ Retrouvez le métier qui correspond à chaque lieu de travail.

Aide
Servez-vous des métiers cités à la page 8.

1. She works in the street.
→ ....
2. He/She paints.
→ ....
3. He works in a garage.
→ ....
4. He/She works in a hospital.
→ ....
5. He/She works in a supermarket.
→ ....
6. He/She is at the head of a big company.
→ ....
7. He works on a boat.
→ ....
8. He/She works in a kitchen.
→ ....
9. He/She works in a police station.
→ ....
10. He/She works in a restaurant.
→ ....
11. He/She works in a research centre.
→ ....
12. He/She works in an office, in a factory.
→ ....
13. He/She works in a hotel.
→ ....
14. He/She works in a shop.
→ ....
15. He/She works in a bank, at the post office, etc.
→ ....

2 ★ Reliez les métiers et les activités qui leur correspondent.

1. A nurse •	• a. makes experiments.
2. A mechanic •	• b. works behind a counter.
3. A cook •	• c. repairs cars and vans.
4. A receptionist •	• d. takes care of patients.
5. A scientist •	• e. welcomes people.
6. A shop assistant •	• f. prepares meals.
7. A cashier •	• g. helps children cross the street.
8. A traffic warden •	• h. wraps parcels.

3 ★★ En utilisant le vocabulaire du tableau de la page 8, imaginez ce qui s'est passé dans la vie de Peter aux dates suivantes.

2024 : ....
....
2082 : ....
....
2000 : ....
....
2023 : ....
....
2030 : ....
....

4 ★★★ En reprenant les éléments de l'exercice 3, racontez la vie de Peter chronologiquement et en ajoutant des mots de liaison.

....
....
....
....
....
....
....

Auto évaluation — Très bien ☐ Bien ☐ Pas assez bien ☐

4 Environnement et voyages
Environment and travelling

→ Corrigés p. I

Observer et retenir

At home

Getting up

1. a ladder
2. a staircase (step by step)
3. a lift

Cleaning up

1. a sink
2. a tap
3. a towel
4. a bin

Going outside

1. the roof
2. the chimney
3. the lawn
4. the gate
5. a lawnmower

In town

1. railings
2. park
3. block
4. pavement
5. store
6. subway/tube
7. bench
8. pedestrian crossing
9. petrol station
10. traffic lights

Travelling

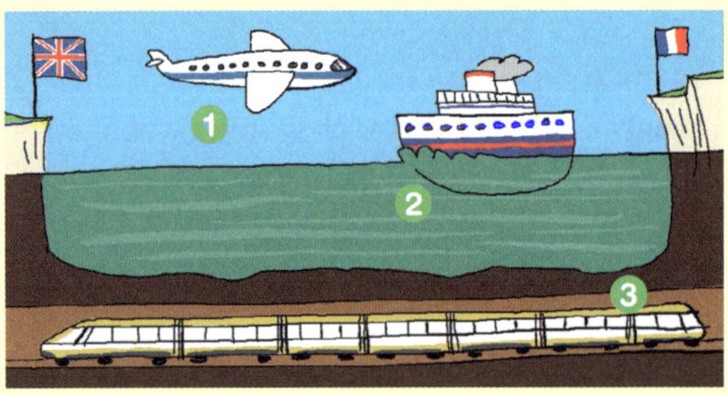

1. **Above:** by plane
2. **On:** by boat (or ferry-boat)
3. **Under:** by train (The Eurostar)

Are you airsick?
Are you seasick?
Have you got a single ticket or a return ticket?

In any case, don't forget your passport or your driving licence and show it at the customs.
The customs officer checks the luggage.

1. the customs officer
2. a case
3. the passenger

S'entraîner

1 ★ Entourez l'intrus dans les propositions suivantes.

1. bin – towel – sink – tap – tip
2. chimney – door – drawer – roof – window
3. ladder – lawn – lift – staircase – step
4. bathroom – bed – makeup – towel – washbasin
5. lift – grass – lawn – mow – tree
6. street – store – house – railings – flowers
7. pedestrian – train – boat – plane – car
8. case – passport – ticket – bin – bag

2 ★★ Répondez aux questions suivantes. Faites des phrases complètes.

1. If you want to have a rest, where can you go?

....

2. If you want to buy all sorts of things, where do you go?

....

3. Where is it pleasant to sit in the park?

....

4. Where do pedestrians walk?

....

5. Where must you cross the street?

....

6. What is the fastest means of transport in big towns?

....

7. In the tube, what are the walls covered with?

....

8. When the lights are red, what must car drivers do?

....

9. There are no cottages in town! What do people live in?

....

10. What is a park surrounded by?

....

3 ★★ Parmi les mots proposés, choisissez ceux qui se rapportent aux voyages en voiture, en bateau ou en avion.

seasick – speed – driving licence – take off – petrol station – crossing – flight – fly – ship – brake – waves – land – fasten – car-ferry – map – airport – airbag – sea

Car: ....

....

Boat: ....

....

Plane: ....

....

4 ★★★ Complétez les phrases suivantes avec l'une des deux propositions indiquées.

1. The car driver was in a hurry but he (accelerated/braked) .... at the lights.
2. At the airport Mr Smith (checked in/flew) .... at the counter.
3. He could not take his plane because (the flight was cancelled/there was a lot of information) ....
4. When he arrived at Heathrow he (got in/got off) .... the plane.
5. Mrs Jones travelled by ferry. She (flew/sailed) .... across the Channel.
6. The ferry was late; so she (caught/missed) .... the train to London.
7. The driver drove too fast; he was (stopped/encouraged) .... by the police.
8. Cars must stop when the traffic lights are (red/green).................................. .

Auto évaluation Très bien ☐ Bien ☐ Pas assez bien ☐

5 La nature, les animaux
Nature, animals

→ Corrigés p. I

Observer et retenir

Nature

1. wood
2. hill
3. lake
4. branch
5. leaf

1. beach
2. shore
3. waves
4. island

Climate

January

The wind **blows**.
It is **icy** (as cold as ice).
It **freezes** (under 0°).

August

Look at the **flash of lightning**.
Listen to the **clap of thunder**.
It is very hot and **stormy**.

November

It is **misty** (you can't see very well).
It is **chilly** (not very warm).
Winter is coming.

Animals

a bear

a buffalo

a butterfly

a frog

a guinea-pig

a monkey

a mouse

a snake

a spider

a wolf

S'entraîner

1 ★ Répondez aux questions suivantes.

1. What is smaller than a forest? ……………………
2. What is smaller than a mountain? ……………………
3. What is green in spring and yellow in autumn? ……………………
4. Where can leaves be seen? ……………………

2 ★ À quels mots (anglais) présentés page 12 les mots suivants vous font-ils penser ?

1. Robinson Crusoé → ……………………
2. Naufrage → ……………………
3. Vacances → ……………………
4. Mer → ……………………

3 ★★ Que se passe-t-il chaque mois ? Assemblez les propositions des deux colonnes et reportez les résultats dans la grille ci-dessous.

1. In January…
2. In February…
3. In March…
4. In April…
5. In May…
6. In June…
7. In July…
8. In August…
9. In September…
10. In October…
11. In November…
12. In December…

a. … it's Halloween time.
b. … cherries are red.
c. … school starts, with autumn!
d. … it is hot and stormy.
e. … the weather is still icy.
f. … cold weather comes back.
g. … the first day is a holiday.
h. … it often snows.
i. … leaves begin to fall.
j. … it rains regularly.
k. … mornings are still usually chilly.
l. … children enjoy their holidays.

1	2	3	4	5	6	7	8	9	10	11	12

4 ★★★ Complétez la grille de mots croisés en vous aidant du vocabulaire de la leçon, p.12.

Attention
Les définitions sont en français, les mots à trouver en anglais.

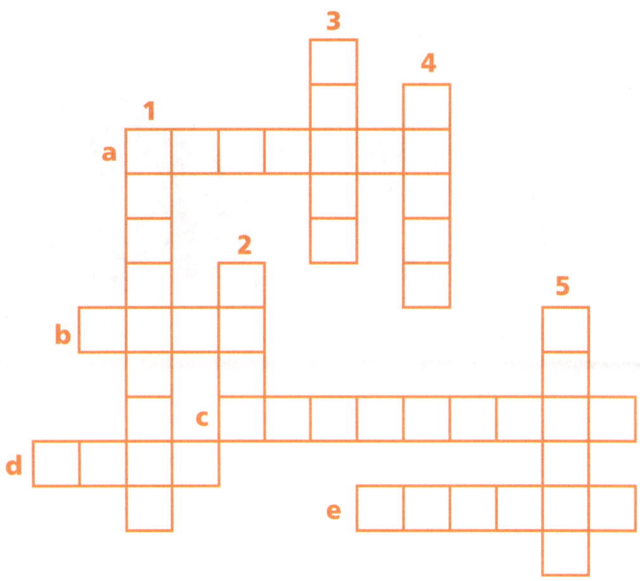

Down
1. Vole de fleur en fleur.
2. Nourriture des Français… disent les Anglais.
3. Son venin est dangereux.
4. Mickey, Minnie, etc.
5. Tisse sa toile.

Across
a. Chassé par le colonel Cody… et les Indiens.
b. Hiberne l'hiver.
c. Animal de compagnie.
d. L'ennemi des trois petits cochons.
e. Mange des bananes.

Auto évaluation Très bien ☐ Bien ☐ Pas assez bien ☐

6 Les relations
Relationships

→ Corrigés p. I

Observer et retenir

Attitude

Peter is very nice	
He always **agrees with** everybody.	= He always says "yes".
He loves **chatting** with friends.	= He loves talking for hours.
He **gets on well with** everybody.	= He is friendly.
He **congratulates** his friends on their success.	= He tells his friends: "I'm very glad for you."
He **hugs** his parents when he comes back home.	= He takes his parents in his arms when he comes back.
He always **tells the truth**.	= What he says is never false.
He **shares** his things with the others.	= He lends or gives his things.
He always gives **friendly** looks to people.	
He is rather **shy**.	= He is timid.
He is **polite**.	
So his parents **allow** him to go out on Saturday nights.	

Gerald is horrible
He always **disagrees with** everybody.
He always **argues with** everybody.
He **quarrels** all the time.
He **blames** everybody.
He **hits** everybody.
He keeps **lying**.
He **keeps** everything **for** himself.
He always gives **cross** looks to people.
He is **cheeky**.
He is **rude**.
So his parents **oblige** him to stay at home on Saturday nights.

How to be polite

Happy birthday!

Pardon me?

Cheers!

– Thank you.
– You're welcome.

How to write a letter

At the beginning	→	**At the end**
Dear Sir,	→	Yours sincerely.
Dear parents,	→	Lots of love.
Dear Susie,	→	Take care! All the best! Best wishes!

S'entraîner

1 ★ Trouvez les deux mots qui se cachent dans chaque suite de lettres.

Aide
Tous les mots figurent à la page 14.

1. AACEGHRTU
→ .... → ....
2. GHHITU
→ .... → ....
3. DEEILOPRTU
→ .... → ....
4. CEEHHKSYY
→ .... → ....
5. ABEGILLLOOW
→ .... → ....
6. CDEFILNORRSSY
→ .... → ....

2 ★★ Complétez ces phrases en utilisant l'un des deux mots proposés. Attention au sens !

1. When you get a good mark your teacher (congratulates/blames) .... you.
2. When you see a spider you are (pleased/frightened) ....
3. People who are cross (quarrel/get on well) .... with their neighbours.
4. If you are generous, you (share/keep) .... what you have with the others.
5. When you don't want to say that you didn't go to school you (lie/tell the truth) ....
6. When you get red easily it shows you are (timid/ cheeky) ....
7. When you say "Thank you", you are (polite/rude) ....

3 ★★★ À travers ces situations simples se révèle le caractère de celui qui parle. Pour caractériser son attitude, utilisez les phrases clés qui se trouvent page 14.

1. I don't think Susie is right. And Christopher is certainly wrong. I can't accept what Paul says.
→ ....
2. Good morning, Mr Jones. How are you, Mrs Jones? I hope you feel better, Sandy.
→ ....
3. Bloody restaurant! I ain't going to swallow all that stuff.
→ ....
4. Bless you, Vicki! Cheers! I wish you a very happy birthday!
→ ....
5. I won't tell them... Let me think... I'll tell them the teacher kept us in for an extra two hours.
→ ....
6. Do you want to read this book? Yes? Here you are. You can keep it. I've already read it twice.
→ ....
7. I'm so glad you passed the test. It's a great step forward. Bravo!
→ ....
8. Andrew shouldn't have done that! And Mary shouldn't have agreed with him. To say nothing of their parents who can't do things properly.
→ ....
9. When I meet them, I'll strike as much as I can. I'll slap James on his face and I'll knock down Albert.
→ ....
10. Oh, no, I can't face all these people. I'll never be able to shake hands with them. I feel terrified. I'll hide behind the door.
→ ....

Auto évaluation Très bien ☐ Bien ☐ Pas assez bien ☐

7 La pensée, les sentiments
Thought, feelings

→ Corrigés p. I

Observer et retenir

Adjectives

ashamed

mad

worried

frightened

enthusiastic

embarrassed

determined

nervous

A **careless** driver.

Guilty!

Isn't she **attractive**?

She's **in trouble**.

Verbal expressions

be interested (*s'intéresser à*)	John is interested **in** making model planes.
complain (*se plaindre de*)	Lucy is always complaining **about** food.
enjoy (*bien aimer*)	Peter enjoys parties.
	William enjoys sleep**ing** in the open air.
expect (*s'attendre à*)	Betty is not good at English. I expect **her to** work more.
forget (*oublier*)	Jack is so absent-minded that he always forgets his keys.
mind (*être gêné*)	Do you mind **my** com**ing** with you?
notice (*remarquer*)	I didn't notice the car.
	I didn't notice **that** the traffic lights were red.
remind (*rappeler*)	This bright boy reminds me **of** Harry Potter.
	He reminded me **of** post**ing** my letter.
succeed (*réussir à*)	Betty succeeded **in** her exam.
	Betty succeeded **in** gett**ing** good marks.
wonder (*se demander*)	I wonder **if** the weather will be fine tomorrow.

S'entraîner

1 ★ Complétez les phrases suivantes en choisissant, parmi les trois adjectifs qui vous sont proposés, celui qui correspond à la situation évoquée.

1. *Ashamed – frightened – worried* : When watching that horror film, Linda was really ....

2. *Determined – ashamed – enthusiastic* : Susan was .... to be invited to a rock concert. She had never been there before.

3. *Determined – nervous – worried* : Bob practised the piano every day because he was .... to play in concerts.

4. *Attractive – careless – mad* : Look at this lovely girl. She is so .... that all the boys fall in love with her.

5. *Guilty – ashamed – determined* : Fred had lied to his parents. He was so .... that he got red in the face.

6. *Careless – guilty – nervous* : Margaret panics easily; she is always .... before an exam.

2 ★★ Trouvez les verbes correspondant aux situations suivantes.

1. My bed is hard. I haven't got my breakfast.

→ ....

2. She had great fun at the party yesterday evening.

→ ....

3. He bumped into a lamp-post. He hadn't seen it!

→ ....

4. Shall we go to the cinema or to the theatre? I'm not sure.

→ ....

5. Where are my keys? I must have left them in the car.

→ ....

6. Betty has got good marks.

→ ....

3 ★★★ Inventez des phrases en utilisant les constructions verbales suivantes.

1. Complain about (+ *nom*)

→ ....

....

2. Remind someone of (something *ou base verbale* + ing)

→ ....

....

3. Forget (something *ou* that + *proposition*)

→ ....

....

4. Enjoy (+ *nom ou base verbale* + -ing)

→ ....

....

5. Expect someone (to do something)

→ ....

....

6. Be interested in (+ *nom ou base verbale* + -ing)

→ ....

....

7. Succeed in (+ *nom ou base verbale* + -ing)

→ ....

....

8. Wonder (if + *proposition*)

→ ....

....

9. Notice (+ *nom ou proposition introduite par* that)

→ ....

....

10. Mind (+ *adjectif possessif* + *base verbale* + -ing)

→ ....

....

Auto évaluation — Très bien ☐ Bien ☐ Pas assez bien ☐

8 Les institutions, le commerce
Institutions, commerce

→ Corrigés p. I

Observer et retenir

Institutions

The Queen of England reigns over the United Kingdom and the Commonwealth.

The Parliament is composed of:
- the House of Lords;
- the House of Commons.

The Prime Minister is appointed by the Queen.

M.P.s (Members of Parliament) are elected to the House of Commons.

The President of the United States of America is elected for four years.

The Congress is composed of:
- the Senate;
- the House of Representatives.

All members of Congress are elected.

Commerce

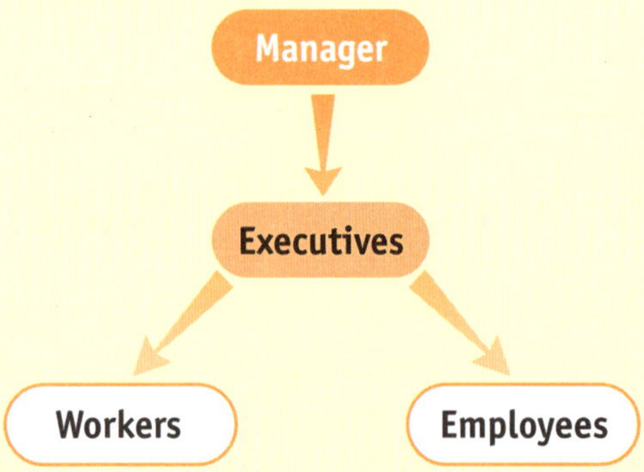

The staff of a company

The staff of a shop

In the shop

CUSTOMER: Could I have it right now?

SHOP ASSISTANT: Sorry, Sir. We're **short of** them. I have to **order** some.

CUSTOMER: Could I have them next Monday, then?

SHOP ASSISTANT: No, Sir. Monday is a **bank holiday**. The shop is closed.

CUSTOMER: What about Tuesday?

SHOP ASSISTANT: Awfully sorry, Sir. But it's my **day off**. I don't work on Tuesdays.

CUSTOMER: That's what is called a "**full-time**" job.

SHOP ASSISTANT: No, Sir. I'm just here for two weeks. I've only got a "**part-time**" job!

S'entraîner

1 ★ Pour remplir ces mots croisés, retrouvez qui a prononcé ces phrases.

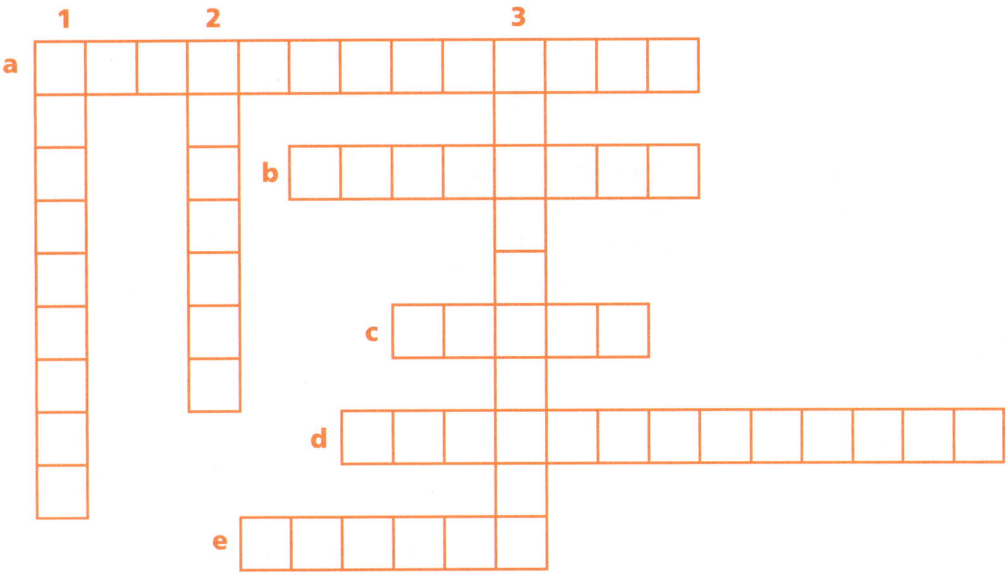

Down

1. I've been elected for four years.
2. My executives will meet next week.
3. My shop must be painted again.

Across

a. I want this law to be voted.
b. I'd like to buy a dress.
c. Where's my crown?
d. Can I help you?
e. I'm fed up with working on this machine all day.

2 ★★ Dans ce dialogue, imaginez les questions de Luke.

1. LUKE: .... ?
   EMILY: Yes, Luke, London has a mayor.
2. LUKE: .... ?
   EMILY: Practically all the capitals of Europe have got their mayors.
3. LUKE: .... ?
   EMILY: He should be elected.
4. LUKE: .... ?
   EMILY: For four years.
5. LUKE: .... ?
   EMILY: By all the inhabitants of London.
6. LUKE: .... ?
   EMILY: He works in City Hall.

3 ★★★ Corrigez les erreurs qui se sont glissées dans ces phrases.

1. A shopkeeper owns a company.
   → ....
2. At the head of a firm there is an employee.
   → ....
3. An executive works in a shop.
   → ....
4. The manager is helped by several shop assistants.
   → ....
5. Employees work on a bank holiday.
   → ....

Auto évaluation Très bien ☐ Bien ☐ Pas assez bien ☐

9 La négation, l'interrogation

→ Corrigés p. II

Observer et retenir

Miss Question, Mr No and Mr Yes

MISS QUESTION: **Do you like** going to the cinema?

MR NO: No, **I don't**.

MISS QUESTION: **Would you like** to see a good film with me, Mr Yes?

MR YES: Oh, yes, with pleasure.

MISS QUESTION: Where and when **could we meet**?

MR YES: We **could meet** at the cinema, at 6 p.m. I'**m** never late.

Remarque
Voir aussi fiche 37 « Les mots interrogatifs ».

■ **L'ordre des mots**

	Négation	Interrogation
Temps simples (verbes ordinaires)	sujet + *do* (*does*, *did*) + *not* + base verbale	*do* (*does*, *did*) + sujet + base verbale… ?
Temps composés	sujet + *have* (*has*) + *not* + p. passé	*have* (*has*) + sujet + p. passé… ?
Modaux	sujet + modal + *not* + base verbale	modal + sujet + base verbale… ?

■ Dans les **questions « ouvertes »**, un **mot interrogatif** précède les structures indiquées ci-dessus.

■ **Exemple de question fermée :** *Did you go to the cinema last month?*

■ **Exemple de question ouverte :** *How many times did you go to the cinema last month?*

S'entraîner

1 ★ Transformez les phrases suivantes en les mettant à la forme négative (a) et à la forme interrogative (b).

1. People like living in town.

a. ……………………………………………

b. ……………………………………………

2. I can travel without a case.

a. ……………………………………………

b. ……………………………………………

2 ★★ Remettez les mots dans l'ordre pour faire des phrases négatives ou interrogatives.

1. been – dentist's – has – Mary – never – the – to.

→ ……………………………………………

2. children – Disney – their – visit – will – World – ?

→ ……………………………………………

3. did – last – match – the – watch – week – you – ?

→ ……………………………………………

3 ★★★ Posez les questions portant sur les mots soulignés.

1. My friends go to the cinema <u>during the holidays</u>.

→ ……………………………………………

2. Aston Villa won <u>the Cup</u>.

→ ……………………………………………

3. It takes <u>two hours</u> to go to London.

→ ……………………………………………

Auto évaluation Très bien ☐ Bien ☐ Pas assez bien ☐

10 Présent simple, présent en *-ing*

→ Corrigés p. II

Observer et retenir

A matter of shoes

MOTHER: Good morning. We **want** another pair of shoes.

SHOE-SHOP ASSISTANT: Really?

SON: **I'm not wearing** those shoes again. They hurt.

MOTHER: **He's always complaining**. He **usually wears** sneakers, you know.

SHOE-SHOP ASSISTANT: Anyway, let's try on these shoes. They'll fit you very well.

Présent simple	Présent en *-ing*
■ **L'habitude** **Ex. :** *He usually* ***wears*** *sneakers.* ■ Certains verbes : *want, like, remember, see, hear,* etc. (Voir aussi fiches 13, 14, 22.)	■ La **description** d'une image, d'une situation **Ex. :** *Look! The shoes he* ***is wearing*** *are too tight.* ■ La **position, ex. :** *He* ***is standing****.* ■ **L'agacement, ex. :** *He's always* ***complaining****.* ■ **L'intention, ex. :** ***I'm not wearing*** *those shoes again.*

S'entraîner

1 ★ Si vous aviez à traduire les phrases suivantes, utiliseriez-vous le présent simple ou le présent en *-ing* ? Écrivez P. S. ou P. *-ing* à la fin des phrases suivantes.

1. Regarde ! Elle porte des chaussures à talons. ....
2. Où habites-tu ? ....
3. Tu mâches tout le temps du chewing-gum. ....
4. J'aime le chocolat. ....
5. Je vais à la piscine tous les mardis. ....

2 ★★ Complétez soit avec un présent simple, soit avec un présent en *-ing*. Entourez la solution correcte.

1. When she goes to the restaurant, she (always sits/is always sitting) at the same table.
2. I (don't spend/'m not spending) my holidays in that horrible place anymore.
3. He (buys/is buying) a new car every year.
4. Look at this photo! Everybody (smiles/is smiling) on it.
5. Here the wind (blows/is blowing) seven days a week!

3 ★★★ Traduisez les phrases suivantes.

1. Je ne bois jamais de chocolat le matin.

→ ....

....

2. Écoute ! Il joue du violon aujourd'hui.

→ ....

....

3. Je vois les enfants. Ils sont allongés sur la pelouse.

→ ....

....

4. J'ai honte. Ma fille pleure toujours pour un rien.

→ ....

....

5. Il pleut souvent quand je veux sortir.

→ ....

....

Auto évaluation Très bien ☐ Bien ☐ Pas assez bien ☐

11 Simple past, passé en *-ing*

→ Corrigés p. II

Observer et retenir

Haunted by a bell

When Judith **came** back home, the church bell **struck** twelve. She **sat** down and **turned** on the television. While she **was watching** a horror film the church bell **struck** twelve again. While she **was having** a good time in her cosy house, it **was pouring** outside. When the film **was** over, she **decided** to go to bed… and the church bell **struck** twelve again. And it **did** so every quarter of an hour. Judith **thought**: "If I **were** on a desert island, I would not hear that crazy bell anymore." And she **began** to pack up…

■ Le ***simple past*** s'utilise :

- dans une **biographie**

Exemple *Shakespeare **lived** in Stratford for 24 years.*

- dans un **récit**

Exemple *She **sat** down and **turned** on the television.*

- dans une **hypothèse**

Exemple *If I **were** on a desert island…*

■ Le **passé en *-ing*** s'utilise :

- pour une **action en déroulement continu**

Exemple *While she **was watching** a horror film…*

- pour **deux actions en déroulement continu**

Exemple *While she **was having** a good time…*
*… it **was pouring** outside.*

S'entraîner

1 ★ Répondez aux questions suivantes.

1. What happened when Judith came back home?

→ ....

2. What did she do then?

→ ....

3. Was she having a good time watching television?

→ ....

2 ★ Complétez l'histoire en mettant les verbes indiqués au passé simple ou au passé en *-ing*.

Willy (be) .... in a hurry and so (be) .... the dog. A fat man (run) .... after the dog. The big black dog (crash) .... into Willy's bicycle. "That dog… I'll kill it," the fat man (say) .... "Me too," (say) .... Willy as he (get) .... to his feet. "Is it your dog?"
"It's not my dog and your bicycle (fall) .... into pieces anyway. I (work) .... on the road and I (just sit down) .... when the dog (come along) .... I (have) .... my ham sandwich when the dog (snatch) .... it away from my hand." Willy (look) .... at the wheels when the big black dog (come) .... back.

Adapted from *The School at Ash Green* by W. C. H. Chalk.

3 ★★★ Utilisez une des deux formes du passé pour compléter les phrases suivantes.

1. Willy (fall) .... from his bicycle and he (feel) .... stupid.
2. He (become) .... a doctor and (begin) .... a bright career.
3. The dog (bite) .... Willy while he (beat) .... it.

Auto évaluation Très bien ☐ Bien ☐ Pas assez bien ☐

12 Present perfect

→ Corrigés p. II

Observer et retenir

A bad secretary

The boss: **Have** you ever **worked** as a secretary?

Secretary: Yes, I have.

The boss: **Have** you **been typing** this morning?

Secretary: Yes, of course.

The boss: How many letters **have** you **typed**?

Secretary: Ten.

The boss: **Have** you **typed** the letter to Mr Smith?

Secretary: Sorry, I **haven't had** the time to do it yet.

The boss: My goodness! **Have** you ever **realised** the meaning of "urgent"? You are fired.

■ Le *present perfect* simple (*have* + participe passé) exprime un bilan fait dans le présent d'évènements passés.

Exemple *Have you ever **worked** as a secretary?*

■ Le *present perfect* en *-ing* (*have been* + base verbale + *-ing*) insiste sur l'activité et non sur l'évènement.

Exemple ***Have** you **been typing** this morning?*

■ Le *present perfect* se combine avec *just*, *ever*, *never* et *yet*.

Exemples *He has **just** finished typing.* (Il vient de s'arrêter de taper à la machine.)
*Have you **ever** worked as a secretary?* (Avez-vous déjà travaillé comme secrétaire ?) *I've **never** worked as a secretary.* (Je n'ai jamais travaillé comme secrétaire.)
*I have **not** had the time **yet**.* (Je n'ai pas encore eu le temps.)

S'entraîner

1 ★ Mettez les verbes entre parenthèses au *present perfect* simple.

1. Philip (be) .... to the States twice.
2. I (think) .... about it.
3. What (eat) ....? Your lips are red.
4. (finish) .... you .... reading this book?

2 ★★ Trouvez les questions portant sur les mots soulignés.

1. Yes, I've seen all the monuments of London.
→ ....
2. I've just visited the British Museum.
→ ....
3. Yes, I've sent a lot of postcards to my friends this morning.
→ ....
4. I've been sightseeing this morning.
→ ....
5. No, I haven't been disappointed up to now.
→ ....

3 ★★★ Traduisez les phrases suivantes.

1. As-tu déjà pris ton petit déjeuner ?
→ ....
2. Il est onze heures et je n'ai pas encore pris mon petit déjeuner.
→ ....
3. As-tu déjà pris un petit déjeuner anglais ?
→ ....
4. Non, je n'en ai jamais pris.
→ ....

Auto évaluation Très bien ☐ Bien ☐ Pas assez bien ☐

13 For, during, since

→ Corrigés p. II

Observer et retenir

A new salesman

AMY: **Have you always worked** as a salesman?

OLIVER: No, I **worked** as a waiter **for** two years. Then I **worked** at McDonald's **during** the summer holidays.

AMY: **Have you found** a job **since** then?

OLIVER: Unfortunately no. I **have been unemployed for** six months, **since** the first of September.

AMY: Strange! **We've been looking** for a salesman **for** six months, and here you are!

■ ***Since*** (depuis) : *present perfect* + *since* + date précise.

Exemple *I've been unemployed **since** the first of September.*

■ ***For*** (depuis) : *present perfect* + *for* + durée (état, action inachevée).

Exemple *I've been unemployed **for** six months.*

■ ***For*** (pendant) : prétérit + *for* + durée (état, action révolue).

Exemple *I worked there **for** two years.*

Remarques

- ***For*** est suivi d'une précision chiffrée (*for six months, for two years*).
- ***During*** est suivi d'une précision non chiffrée (*during the summer holidays*).

S'entraîner

1 ★ Entourez la phrase française qui rend compte du sens de la phrase anglaise.

1. I worked as a waiter for two years.
   a. *Il est toujours serveur.*
   b. *Il n'est plus serveur.*
2. I looked for a job for six months.
   a. *Il a trouvé du travail.*
   b. *Il n'a toujours pas trouvé de travail.*
3. I've been unemployed for six months.
   a. *Maintenant il a un travail.*
   b. *Il n'a toujours pas de travail.*
4. We've been looking for a salesman for six months.
   a. *Elle a trouvé un vendeur.*
   b. *Elle cherche toujours un vendeur.*
5. I was unemployed for six months.
   a. *Il n'a pas travaillé pendant six mois.*
   b. *Il travaille depuis six mois.*

2 ★★ Complétez les phrases suivantes avec *for*, *since* ou *during* suivant le cas.

1. What have you been doing .... the holidays?
2. What have you been doing .... the beginning of the holidays?
3. This boat has sailed .... two weeks.
4. At that time, we stayed in London .... a month.
5. .... July we've been living in Paris.

3 ★★★ Imaginez la fin de ces phrases.

1. Has he been your friend for .... ?
2. He's been my friend since ....
3. I met him during ....
4. Did you see him during .... ?
5. I haven't seen him for ....

Auto évaluation Très bien ☐ Bien ☐ Pas assez bien ☐

14 L'expression du futur

→ Corrigés p. II

Observer et retenir

Planning a party

BETTY: What **are you doing** on Friday night?

SALLY: I don't know yet. What about giving a party?

BETTY: Yes! **I'll invite** all my friends. Dad, **we're going to** have a party! When **do you finish** working on Friday?

DAD: I **finish** at four, but remember **I'm leaving** early next Saturday.

BETTY: Don't worry, Dad. The party **won't finish** too late.

Le **futur** peut s'exprimer de **quatre façons** :

- *Be* + base verbale + *-ing* + marqueur de temps → ***I'm leaving** early next Saturday.*

= Décision personnelle. Le père partira au moment qu'il a fixé.

- Présent simple → *I **finish** at four.*

= Décision extérieure. Il quittera son bureau à l'heure imposée de fermeture.

- *Will* + base verbale → ***I'll invite** all my friends.*

= Décision prise à l'instant. On lui propose une soirée ; immédiatement elle pense à inviter tous ses amis.

Remarque
'll = will ; won't = will + not.

- *Be going to* + base verbale → ***We're going to have** a party.*

= Décision prise antérieurement. Betty informe son père de la décision que Sally vient de prendre.

S'entraîner

1 ★ Entourez la forme verbale qui convient.

1. At school, what time (do you start – are you starting – will you start) on Monday morning?

2. Next year Henry (ski – is skiing – is going to ski) in the Alps.

3. Don't move! (I'm going to open – I'll open – I'm opening) the door.

4. This young couple (will buy – is going to buy – is buying) a house as soon as they can. They have just told me.

5. Tomorrow she (will take – is taking – takes) an early train.

2 ★★ Complétez les phrases suivantes avec le verbe proposé, décliné au futur avec *will* ou *be going to*.

1. I haven't got any money. – Don't worry! I (give) .... you some.

2. I (be) .... 16 tomorrow.

3. The teacher said: "Today we (listen) .... to a recording."

4. Did you buy some bread? – Sorry! I (do) .... it now.

5. What a beautiful sun! I (sit) .... under this big tree.

3 ★★★ Sur une feuille à part, traduisez les phrases suivantes.

1. Vous trouverez une boulangerie au coin de la rue.

2. Il fait chaud. Je vais ouvrir la fenêtre.

3. Mary va avoir un bébé.

Auto évaluation Très bien ☐ Bien ☐ Pas assez bien ☐

15 La condition, l'hypothèse

→ Corrigés p. II

Observer et retenir

Dreams

William is day-dreaming…

… If I **find** a one-pound note, I'**ll buy** some sweets.

… If I **found** a wallet full of banknotes, I'**d buy** a scooter.

… If I **found** a treasure, I'**d buy** an island.

… If I **had** an island, I'**d get** there with my sweets and my moped.

… If I **were** as rich as that, **would** I really **be** happy?

Remarque

Ces « passés simples » s'appellent des « **prétérits modaux** ».
Were à toutes les personnes est le prétérit modal de *be*.

■ La **condition** implique que l'évènement peut se produire.

If I ***find*** *a one-pound note, I* ***'ll buy*** *some sweets.*

find ↑ ***Présent simple*** — ***'ll buy*** ↑ ***Will*** **+ base verbale**

■ L'**hypothèse** implique que l'évènement pourrait se réaliser… ou qu'il est irréalisable !

If I ***found*** *a wallet…, I* ***'d buy*** *a scooter.*

found ↑ ***Simple past*** — ***'d buy*** ↑ ***Would*** **+ base verbale**

S'entraîner

1 ★ Complétez les phrases suivantes qui expriment la condition (phrases 1, 2, 3) ou l'hypothèse (phrases 4, 5, 6).

1. If Philip (work) .... well, his father (give) .... him a bike.
2. If he (marry) .... a duchess, he (live) .... in a castle.
3. If the weather (be) .... fine, I (go and see) .... my neighbour.
4. If Mary (be not) .... always late, her teacher (be) .... glad.
5. If men (can) .... fly, what (become) .... birds ....?
6. If nobody (smoke) .... , we (breathe) .... better.

2 ★★ Reliez les propositions de la première colonne à des propositions de la seconde colonne pour construire des phrases ayant un sens.

1. If I find a nice flat… •	• a. … they would be furious.
2. If I didn't go to their party… •	• b. … I would be scared.
3. If you lie… •	• c. … I'll buy it.
4. If I climbed up Mount Blanc… •	• d. … they would fly.
5. If pigs had wings… •	• e. … what would you do?
6. If you were lost in a forest… •	• f. … you'll be punished.

Auto évaluation Très bien ☐ Bien ☐ Pas assez bien ☐

16 Capacité, possibilité, permission

→ Corrigés p. II

Observer et retenir

Help!

DRIVER: My car is broken. **Could** you help me?

HORRIBLE MAN: No. I've no time… It **may** rain… You **can** manage by yourself.

NICE MAN: **May** I borrow your hammer? I think I **can** repair your car.

DRIVER: Thank you. That's very kind of you.

HORRIBLE MAN (*aside*): They won't **be able to** do it.

■ *Can* et *may* sont des verbes modaux, donc **invariables**.

■ ***Can***

- Il sert à exprimer une **capacité physique** ou **intellectuelle**.

Exemple *You can manage.*

- Son passé *could* exprime les mêmes capacités. Il traduit le passé et le conditionnel.
- Aux autres temps que le présent et le passé, on utilise *be able to*.
- *Could* introduit une **question polie**.

Exemple *Could you help me?*

■ ***May***

- Il exprime la **permission** ou la **demande de permission**.

Exemple *May I borrow your hammer?*

- Il exprime aussi l'**éventualité** (3e personne neutre).

Exemple *It may rain.*

S'entraîner

1 ★ Quelle est la valeur de *can* dans les phrases suivantes ? Cochez dans le tableau.

1. Could you tell me the way to the station?
2. I can speak Chinese, you know.
3. Elephants can draw big trees in India.
4. Peter could work better if he wanted to.

Capacité physique	Capacité intellectuelle	Forme de politesse	Valeur de conditionnel

2 ★★ Complétez avec *can* ou *may* suivant le sens de la phrase.

1. My friend Paul .... come this afternoon; he hasn't decided yet.
2. I don't know what .... happen.
3. You .... do this exercise without a dictionary.

3 ★★★ Sur une feuille à part, traduisez les phrases suivantes en utilisant *can*, *could*, *may* ou *be able to*.

1. Si elle va à la campagne, Mary pourra se reposer après le déjeuner.
2. Elle pourrait vendre ses tableaux s'ils étaient moins chers.
3. Cecily a une très belle voix ; il se peut qu'elle devienne chanteuse d'opéra.

Auto évaluation Très bien ☐ Bien ☐ Pas assez bien ☐

17 Incapacité, impossibilité, refus de permission

→ Corrigés p. II

Observer et retenir

Poor boy

SUSAN: What about Jeremy?

JANE: Poor Jeremy! He **can't speak** English properly. He **can't drive in** a nail. His father told me he **couldn't swim** nor ride a bike!

SUSAN: Oh, it **can't be** true!

JANE: And his father keeps telling him: "You **can't grow** flowers on the balcony. You **can't watch** TV after 8 p.m. **You can't**..."

SUSAN: Poor boy! What can we do for him?

■ La forme négative ***can't*** sert à exprimer :

- l'**incapacité intellectuelle** ou **physique**

Exemple *He **can't** speak English properly. He **can't** drive in a nail.*

- l'**impossibilité**

Exemple *It **can't** be true.*

- la **permission non accordée**

Exemple *You **can't** watch television after 8 p.m.*

Remarque
L'absence de permission s'exprime aussi, de façon plus formelle, par ***not to be allowed to***.
Ex. : *Jeremy **is not allowed to** watch television after 8 p.m.*

S'entraîner

1 ★ **Quelle est la valeur de *can't* dans les phrases suivantes ? Cochez la bonne case.**

	Incapacité intellectuelle	Incapacité physique	Impossibilité	Permission non accordée
1. She can't learn mathematics. It's too difficult for her.				
2. He is a liar. She can't stand him.				
3. Old Mr Jones can't go up the stairs anymore.				
4. "Can I park here?" "No, you can't."				
5. He is too honest. He can't be the murderer.				

2 ★★ **Complétez les phrases ci-dessous à l'aide de *can*, *can't*, *could*, *couldn't* suivis d'un de ces verbes : *be*, *put*, *read*.**

1. He was so nervous that he .... the key in the lock.
2. Can you give me my glasses? I .... this article.
3. The French team lost their last match. – It .... true.

3 ★★★ **Traduisez les phrases suivantes.**

1. Vous ne pouvez pas sortir si vous avez de la fièvre. → ....
2. On n'est pas autorisé à fumer au cinéma. → ....
3. Il ne peut pas être à Londres. Je viens de le voir. → ....

Auto évaluation Très bien ☐ Bien ☐ Pas assez bien ☐

18 Obligation, interdiction, forte probabilité

→ Corrigés p. II

Observer et retenir

At school

DAD: How was your first day of school? It **must** have been great to meet new people!

BEN: It was but we **have to** remember a lot of rules! We **mustn't** wear hats in class. We **must** respect the school's dress code but at least **we don't have to** wear a uniform.

■ ***Must*** est un modal qui sert à exprimer :

- une **obligation** ;

Exemple *We **must** respect the school's dress code.*

- une **quasi-certitude**.

Exemple *It **must** have been great to meet new people!*

■ ***Mustn't*** marque l'**interdiction**.

Exemple *We **mustn't** wear hats in class.*

■ ***Have to*** indique généralement une **contrainte** venant de l'extérieur (personne, évènement, règlement).

Exemple *We **have to** remember a lot of rules!*

■ ***Not have to*** indique l'**absence de nécessité**.

Exemple *We **don't have to** wear a uniform.*

Remarques

- ***Have to*** remplace *must* aux autres temps que le présent.
Ex. : *You'll **have to** pass a lot of tests first.*
- On peut aussi utiliser ***be forbidden to*** pour exprimer une très forte interdiction.
Ex. : *It's **forbidden to** smoke here.*
(= No smoking!)

S'entraîner

1 ★ Indiquez les valeurs des verbes soulignés dans les phrases suivantes. Cochez les cases qui conviennent.

1. It's midday. You must be hungry.
2. Everybody is sleeping; you mustn't make any noise.
3. In England, students must wear uniforms.
4. I must stop working if I want to keep fit.
5. You don't have to bring your books; tomorrow there is a test.
6. If you get a job in this company, you won't have to wear a tie.

	obligation		absence d'obligation	interdiction	forte probabilité	autre temps que le présent
	interne	externe				
1.						
2.						
3.						
4.						
5.						
6.						

2 ★★ Complétez les phrases suivantes avec *mustn't*, *do*/*does not have to*, *didn't have to* suivant le sens.

1. You .... to be a genius to use a computer.
2. This is a secret. You .... tell anybody.
3. I told you it was a secret. You .... to tell everybody.

Auto évaluation Très bien ☐ Bien ☐ Pas assez bien ☐

19 Shall/should

→ Corrigés p. II

Observer et retenir

Suggestions

ARTHUR: **Shall we** watch the match on television?

CHRISTOPHER: **Why not** go to the stadium? And **we could** pick up Jenny and Ann on the way.

ARTHUR: All right. Then you should ask your father to drive us there.

CHRISTOPHER: If he doesn't want to, what **about** taking the bus?

ARTHUR: Let's go and see your father first, **shall we**?

■ ***Shall*** est un modal qui, à la 1re personne, sert à **suggérer**, à **proposer**, uniquement à la forme interrogative.

Exemple *__Shall__ we watch the match on television?*

■ Pour **suggérer**, on peut aussi utiliser des expressions telles que :

- ***what about*** + base verbale + ***-ing*** ;
- ***why not*** + base verbale ;
- le modal ***could***.

Exemple *We __could__ pick up Jenny and Ann on the way.*

■ ***Should*** sert à exprimer le **conseil**.

Exemple *You __should__ ask your father.*

■ Le **conseil négatif** se fait avec ***shouldn't***, la forme négative de ***should***.

Exemple *You __shouldn't__ smoke so much.*

À savoir

On est alors très proche du **reproche**.

S'entraîner

1 ★ Un ami va camper en forêt. Donnez-lui cinq conseils positifs et négatifs en utilisant *should* et *shouldn't*.

1. ....
2. ....
3. ....
4. ....
5. ....

2 ★★ Exprimez différemment l'idée contenue dans chacune de ces phrases en en respectant le sens.

1. Let's take a walk, shall we?

→ ....

2. We could have a rest in the forest.

→ ....

3. What about watching the birds?

→ ....

4. Why not have a picnic there?

→ ....

3 ★★★ Suggérez à vos parents un voyage à Londres de cinq façons différentes, en variant chaque fois les arguments et conseils.

1. ....
2. ....
3. ....
4. ....
5. ....

Auto évaluation Très bien ☐ Bien ☐ Pas assez bien ☐

Nouveau
Cahier du jour
Cahier du soir

Corrigés

Corrigés détachables

VOCABULAIRE ET CIVILISATION

1 Le sport et la santé — p. 4

1 **1.** versus (*ou* vs.) – **2.** teams – **3.** attend/seat – **4.** coach; trained – **5.** scoreboard; scored; goals – **6.** support.

2 **1.** I use a shampoo. – **2.** They use a razor (*ou* a shaver). – **3.** I need soap and water. – **4.** They put them in their handbags. – **5.** They use handkerchiefs (hankies). – **6.** They put on earrings. – **7.** It's my/a perfume! – **8.** makeup – **9.** a/my purse. – **10.** a brush.

3 **1.** temperature – **2.** a headache – **3.** disease – **4.** medicines – **5.** rest.

4 **1.** d – **2.** a – **3.** e – **4.** b – **5.** c.

2 La nourriture, le restaurant — p. 6

1 **1.** beef; beer – **2.** coffee; milk – **3.** mushroom; mutton – **4.** strawberry; grapefruit.

2 **1.** fish – **2.** tea – **3.** banana – **4.** carrot – **5.** biscuits – **6.** bottle – **7.** cherry – **8.** toast – **9.** hamburger – **10.** knife.

3 **1.** Could you bring me the menu? – **2.** I'd like to have some water. – **3.** Do you have tomato salad? – **4.** Can I have the bill, please? – **5.** Is the tip included?

4 tomato salad, grated carrots – hard-boiled eggs, fish and chips – French beans, cabbage – ice-cream and custard, pudding.

5 **1.** lemon – **2.** mushroom – **3.** potato – **4.** water.

3 La vie et le travail — p. 8

1 **1.** a traffic warden – **2.** an artist – **3.** a mechanic – **4.** a nurse – **5.** a cashier – **6.** a manager – **7.** a sailor – **8.** a cook – **9.** a detective – **10.** a waiter/a waitress – **11.** a scientist – **12.** an engineer – **13.** a receptionist – **14.** a shop assistant – **15.** a clerk.

2 **1.** d – **2.** c – **3.** f – **4.** e – **5.** a – **6.** h – **7.** b – **8.** g.

3 In 2024 he got married. – In 2082 he died. – In 2000 he was born. – In 2023 he got engaged. – In 2030 he got divorced.

4 Peter was born at the beginning of the new millenium, in 2000. He was still very young in 2023 when he got engaged. But he really wanted to marry Susan as soon as possible and he married her in 2024. In 2030, he got divorced and died in 2082.

4 Environnement et voyages — p. 10

1 **1.** tip – **2.** drawer – **3.** lawn – **4.** bed – **5.** dish – **6.** flowers – **7.** pedestrian – **8.** bin.

2 **1.** I go to the park. – **2.** I go to the store. – **3.** It is pleasant to sit on a bench in the park. – **4.** They walk on the pavement. – **5.** I must cross the street at a pedestrian crossing. – **6.** It is the subway. – **7.** They are covered with posters. – **8.** They must stop. – **9.** They live in blocks… or towers… or skyscrapers. – **10.** It is surrounded by railings.

3 Car: speed, driving licence, petrol station, brake, fasten, map, airbag.

Boat: seasick, crossing, ship, waves, land, car-ferry, sea.

Plane: take off, flight, fly, land, fasten, airport.

4 **1.** braked – **2.** checked in – **3.** the flight was cancelled – **4.** got off – **5.** sailed – **6.** missed – **7.** stopped – **8.** red.

5 La nature, les animaux — p. 12

1 **1.** a wood – **2.** a hill – **3.** a leaf – **4.** on branches.

2 **1.** island – **2.** shore – **3.** beach – **4.** waves.

3 **1.** h – **2.** e – **3.** j – **4.** k – **5.** g – **6.** b – **7.** l – **8.** d – **9.** c – **10.** i – **11.** a – **12.** f.

4 **1.** butterfly – **2.** frog – **3.** snake – **4.** mouse – **5.** spider. **a.** buffalo – **b.** bear – **c.** guinea-pig – **d.** wolf – **e.** monkey.

6 Les relations — p. 14

1 **1.** argue; chat – **2.** hit; hug – **3.** polite; rude – **4.** shy; cheeky – **5.** allow; oblige – **6.** cross; friendly.

2 **1.** congratulates – **2.** frightened – **3.** quarrel – **4.** share – **5.** lie – **6.** timid (*ou* shy) – **7.** polite.

3 **1.** He always disagrees. – **2.** He gets on well with everybody (*ou* : He is friendly). – **3.** He is rude. – **4.** He is polite. – **5.** He lies. – **6.** He shares his things with the others (*ou* : He lends or gives his things). – **7.** He congratulates his friends on their success. – **8.** He blames everybody. – **9.** He hits everybody. – **10.** He is rather shy (*ou* : He is timid).

7 La pensée, les sentiments — p. 16

1 **1.** frightened – **2.** enthusiastic – **3.** determined – **4.** attractive – **5.** ashamed – **6.** nervous.

2 **1.** complain – **2.** enjoy – **3.** notice – **4.** wonder – **5.** forget – **6.** succeed.

3 *Corrigé suggéré :* **1.** Farmers and holidaymakers always complain about the weather. – **2.** She reminded me of cleaning the windows. – **3.** I always forget that I have to learn a lesson for Monday. – **4.** Young people enjoy going to parties where they can enjoy themselves. – **5.** Parents always expect their children to become very important persons (V.I.P.s). – **6.** Most teenagers are interested in computers. – **7.** Actors succeed in learning long texts very quickly. – **8.** Nicky wonders if she is really able to drive a car. – **9.** Paul noticed that Emily had changed her dress. – **10.** Thomas doesn't mind my smoking in his house.

8 Les institutions, le commerce — p. 18

1 **1.** president – **2.** manager – **3.** shopkeeper.

a. Prime Minister – **b.** customer – **c.** Queen – **d.** shop assistant – **e.** worker.

2 *Corrigé suggéré :* **1.** Does London have a mayor? – **2.** What about the other capitals of Europe? – **3.** Is he elected or designated? – **4.** For how long is he elected? – **5.** By whom? – **6.** Where does he work?

3 **1.** A shopkeeper owns a shop. – **2.** At the head of a firm there is a manager. – **3.** A shop assistant works in a shop (*ou* : A manager, executives, employees, workers work in a firm). – **4.** The shopkeeper is helped by several shop assistants (*ou* : The manager is helped by several executives) – **5.** Employees do not work on a bank holiday.

© Cahier du jour/Cahier du soir – Anglais 4e

GRAMMAIRE

9 La négation, l'interrogation — p. 20

1 1. a. People do not like living in town. – b. Do people like living in town?

2. a. I can't travel without a case. – b. Can you travel without a case?

2 1. Mary has never been to the dentist's. – 2. Will their children visit Disney World? – 3. Did you watch the match last week?

3 1. When do your friends go to the cinema? – 2. What did Aston Villa win? – 3. How long does it take to go to London?

10 Présent simple, présent en *-ing* — p. 21

1 1. présent en *-ing* – 2. présent simple – 3. présent en *-ing* – 4. présent simple – 5. présent simple.

2 1. always sits – 2. 'm not spending – 3. buys – 4. is smiling – 5. blows.

3 1. I never drink chocolate in the morning. – 2. Listen! He is playing the violin today. – 3. I can see the children lying on the lawn. 4. – I'm ashamed. My daughter is always crying for nothing. – 5. It often rains when I want to go out.

11 *Simple past*, passé en *-ing* — p. 22

1 1. The church bell struck twelve. – 2. She sat down and turned on the television. – 3. Yes, she was.

2 Willy was in a hurry and so was the dog. A fat man was running after the dog. The big black dog crashed into Willy's bicycle. "That dog… I'll kill it," the fat man said. "Me too," said Willy as he got on to his feet. "Is it your dog?" "It's not my dog and your bicycle was falling into pieces anyway. I was working on the road and I was just sitting down when the dog came along. I was having my ham sandwich when the dog snatched it away from my hand." Willy was looking at the wheels when the big black dog came back.

3 1. fell; felt – 2. became; began – 3. bit; was beating.

12 *Present perfect* — p. 23

1 1. has been – 2. have thought – 3. have you eaten – 4. Have you finished.

2 1. Have you seen all the monuments of London? – 2. What museum have you (just) visited? – 3. Have you sent any postcards to your friends this morning? – 4. What have you been doing this morning? – 5. Have you been disappointed up to now?

3 1. Have you already had your breakfast this morning? – 2. It's eleven o'clock and I have not had my breakfast yet. – 3. Have you ever had an English breakfast? – 4. No, I have never had one.

13 *For, during, since* — p. 24

1 1. b. Il n'est plus serveur. – 2. a. Il a trouvé du travail. – 3. b. Il n'a toujours pas de travail. – 4. b. Elle cherche toujours un vendeur. – 5. a. Il n'a pas travaillé pendant six mois.

2 1. during – 2. since – 3. for – 4. for – 5. since.

3 *Corrigé suggéré :* 1. a long time – 2. the beginning of the year – 3. the flight – 4. the summer holidays – 5. a week.

14 L'expression du futur — p. 25

1 1. do you start – 2. is going to ski – 3. I'll open – 4. will buy – 5. is taking.

2 1. 'll give – 2. 'll be – 3. 're going to listen – 4. 'll do – 5. 'm going to sit.

3 1. You'll find a baker's shop at the corner of the street. – 2. It's hot. I'll open the window. – 3. Mary is going to have a baby.

15 La condition, l'hypothèse — p. 26

1 1. works – will give – 2. marries – will live – 3. is – 'll go and see – 4. weren't – would be – 5. could – would… become? – 6. smoked – would breathe.

2 1. c – 2. a – 3. f – 4. b – 5. d – 6. e.

16 Capacité, possibilité, permission — p. 27

1 1. forme de politesse – 2. capacité intellectuelle – 3. capacité physique – 4. valeur de conditionnel.

2 1. may – 2. may – 3. can.

3 1. If she goes to the country, Mary will be able to have a rest after lunch. – 2. She could sell her paintings if they were cheaper. – 3. Cecily has a beautiful voice; she may become an opera singer.

17 Incapacité, impossibilité, refus de permission — p. 28

1 1. incapacité intellectuelle – 2. impossibilité – 3. incapacité physique – 4. permission non accordée – 5. impossibilité.

2 1. couldn't put – 2. can't read – 3. can't be.

3 1. You can't go out if you have a temperature. – 2. We are not allowed to smoke in a cinema. – 3. He can't be in London. I've just seen him.

18 Obligation, interdiction, forte probabilité — p. 29

1 1. forte probabilité – 2. interdiction – 3. obligation externe – 4. obligation interne – 5. absence d'obligation – 6. autre temps que le présent.

2 1. don't have – 2. mustn't – 3. didn't have.

19 *Shall/should* — p. 30

1 *Corrigé suggéré :* 1. You shouldn't light a fire if the weather is dry. – 2. You shouldn't disturb the animals. – 3. You should bring a torch. – 4. You should stop walking before being too tired. – 5. You should pack up a sleeping bag.

2 *Corrigé suggéré :* 1. What about taking a walk? – 2. Why not have a rest in the forest? – 3. Let's watch the birds, shall we? – 4. We could have a picnic there.

3 *Corrigé suggéré :* 1. Why not go to London? – 2. What about going to the British Museum? – 3. We could visit the Tower of London. – 4. You should be fluent in English. – 5. Let's book our train tickets, shall we?

20 L'infinitif — p. 31

1 1. run – 2. to be – 3. shout – 4. to get – 5. to win.

2 1. him to leave – 2. her to look for – 3. me to borrow – 4. them to limit.

3 1. I'm tired. Let me breathe a little! – 2. Johnny made all his musicians play. – 3. From here I can hear the bells ring. – 4. Our English teacher made us read *Robinson Crusoe*.

21 Le gérondif — p. 32

1 1. listening to – 2. dancing and singing – 3. studying.

Corrigés détachables

© Cahier du jour/Cahier du soir – **Anglais 4e**

2 **1.** to meet – **2.** speak – **3.** queuing – **4.** For calculating – **5.** To type.

3 **1.** is fond of; 'd like – **2.** enjoys – **3.** dreams of/about – **4.** After – **5.** can't bear.

22 *There is/there are* p. 33

1 **1.** there will be – **2.** there was – **3.** there would be – **4.** there were.

2 **1.** are – **2.** must be – **3.** will be – **4.** should be – **5.** would be.

3 **1.** The bus is late; there must be a strike. – **2.** There were a lot of guests at the wedding. – **3.** Are there any garages in this town? – **4.** Is there a pilot in the plane? – **5.** There will be many supporters in the stadium. – **6.** There should be plenty of oranges this year.

23 Les propositions subordonnées de temps p. 34

1 **1.** While – **2.** Just as – **3.** As soon as – **4.** When.

2 **1.** became – **2.** have completed – **3.** was; would exist – **4.** was looking for; offered.

3 **1.** When he was on his island, Robinson Crusoe only had one friend. – **2.** While Robinson was hunting, Friday was cooking. – **3.** Robinson thought: "When a boat arrives, I'll light a big fire." – **4.** Friday thought: "When Robinson has gone, what will happen to me?

24 Le passif p. 35

1 **1.** This student was sent to university by the Head. – **2.** A letter (of recommendation) has been written by the Head. – **3.** She will be heartily welcomed by her new mates. – **4.** I'm sure her work will be appreciated by her new teachers.

2 **1.** has just been hired – **2.** was immediately sent – **3.** will be helped – **4.** must be written – **5.** can be considered.

3 **1.** We are invited this Saturday. – **2.** We'll be waited for at the door. – **3.** Fresh drinks will be served. – **4.** This invitation has been sent/was sent to one hundred people – **5.** They will be welcomed. – **6.** His/her car has been stolen.

25 *So/neither* p. 36

1 **1.** don't you? – **2.** has he? – **3.** do they? – **4.** can't you? – **5.** won't she?

2 **1.** So does Arthur. – **2.** Neither can my mother. – **3.** So did Fred. – **4.** So will I. – **5.** Neither have I.

3 *Corrigé suggéré* : **1.** They were ready to start a war, weren't they? – **2.** They had a lot of weapons, hadn't they? – **3.** They fought with courage, didn't they? – **4.** They can't be beaten, can they?

26 *Some/Any* p. 37

1 **1.** b. – **2.** c. – **3.** d. – **4.** a.

2 **1.** nobody – **2.** any – **3.** any – **4.** any; some – **5.** anybody; anything.

3 **1.** Mary thought she would find somebody to speak to. – **2.** But she couldn't see anybody. – **3.** She had something important to say. – **4.** Anyway she would speak to anybody, somewhere, anywhere.

27 L'article (cas général) p. 38

1 **1.** Ø – a – **2.** Some – **3.** a – **4.** The – Ø – Ø – **5.** Ø – the.

2 **1.** Teenagers – **2.** The teenagers – **3.** The teenagers – **4.** Some teenagers – **5.** the teenagers.

3 **1.** I visited a country, the country I was dreaming of. – **2.** The women of this country wear long skirts. – **3.** I saw some strange animals over there. – **4.** The most extraordinary animal had two heads. – **5.** There were some snakes coming out of its mouth.

28 L'article (cas particuliers) p. 39

1 *Corrigé suggéré* : **1.** Scotland – **2.** The Queen – **3.** coal – **4.** horse races.

2 **1.** the; Ø – **2.** Ø; Ø – **3.** Ø; Ø – **4.** Ø; Ø; the; the – **5.** Ø; Ø.

3 **1.** The Alps spread from France to Austria. – **2.** The sky is clear; Mount Blanc can be seen. – **3.** In this film, she was playing the piano on the beach. – **4.** Some like going to the seaside, others to the mountains. – **5.** The Eiffel tower is the highest tower in Paris.

29 Dénombrables et indénombrables p. 40

1 *Dénombrables* : banana, job, key.

Indénombrables : bread, business, information, music, mutton.

Dénombrables ou indénombrables : noise, room.

2 **1.** is – **2.** is – **3.** are – **4.** have.

3 **1.** a – **2.** a – **3.** Ø – **4.** Ø.

4 **1.** My neighbour has long hair. – **2.** I don't have luck but I have courage. – **3.** What's the news? Buy me a paper, please.

30 Les quantificateurs p. 41

1 **1.** e. – **2.** c. – **3.** d. – **4.** a. – **5.** f. – **6.** b.

2 **1.** enough – **2.** much/a few – **3.** too much – **4.** too many – **5.** much; a few.

3 **1.** I have a few hours to spend with you. – **2.** There are too many football matches on television. – **3.** He made a lot of efforts but he did not make much progress. – **4.** A little kindness is better than a lot of money.

31 Le génitif p. 42

1 **1.** the back of the room – **2.** Peter's book – **3.** the Browns' car – **4.** the boss's office – **5.** the leg of the table – **6.** the painter's brush – **7.** the joys of life – **8.** the top of the mountain – **9.** the traitor's gate – **10.** a three minutes' talk.

2 **1.** Charles and Mary's wedding – **2.** A bus driver's job – **3.** the butcher's, the Smiths' - **4.** a two hours' speech.

3 *Corrigé suggéré* : **1.** Mrs Singleton's – **2.** our neighbours' – **3.** the princess's.

32 Les noms composés p. 43

1 **1.** A washing machine – **2.** A shopping bag – **3.** A wine glass – **4.** A bookshop – **5.** A morning paper.

2 **1.** headache – **2.** health problems – **3.** bank manager – **4.** bank holidays – **5.** income tax – **6.** phone number – **7.** insurance company.

3 **1.** Summer holidays are longer than Easter holidays. – **2.** The garage door is open; the car radio has been stolen. – **3.** What do you like best, love stories or detective novels? – **4.** Will you come back by the evening train or by the night flight?

33 L'exclamation p. 44

1 **1.** We had such nice weather! – **2.** What an unpleasant person! – **3.** What fun Tony had at the funfair! – **4.** You bought such a beautiful car!

2 **1.** such/such a – **2.** so – **3.** such a – **4.** such.

© Cahier du jour/Cahier du soir – Anglais 4e

3 1. How – 2. What a – 3. Such – 4. such a.

4 1. What a bright student! – 2. What horrible weather we had last week! – 3. I have never met such an interesting person. – 4. He is so happy that he sings all the time.

34 Comparatif et superlatif p. 45

1 1. warmer – 2. more expensive – 3. better.

2 1. as intelligent as – 2. heavier than – 3. not as serious as – 4. more crowded… than.

3 1. the fastest – 2. the most successful – 3. more dangerous than – 4. the fattest – 5. as necessary… as.

35 Les adjectifs composés p. 46

1 1. b. A. – 2. c. D. – 3. a. C. – 4. d. B.

2 1. The hare is a fast-running animal. – 2. The giant was a very broad-shouldered man – 3. I wanted a light blue dress. – 4. Nowadays cars are mass-produced.

3 1. long-eared – 2. absent-minded – 3. never-ending – 4. thick-skinned – 5. ice-cold Ø – 6. long-distance Ø.

36 Les adverbes p. 47

1 1. I often park my car in this street. – 2. It is almost ten o'clock. – 3. When summer is over, children can't play any longer.

2 1. I totally agree with you. You're quite right. (*ou* : I quite agree with you. You're totally right.) – 2. He is a very serious student. – 3. Peter is rather lazy, but he sometimes works. – 4. Just a minute! She still has to make up.

3 1. She always walks slowly. – 2. He chooses his vegetables carefully. (*ou* : He carefully chooses his vegetables.) – 3. She has never been to England. Yet she speaks English well. – 4. They often think that English is much more useful.

37 Les mots interrogatifs p. 48

1 1. Two. – 2. Ten miles from here. – 3. For two years. – 4. Mr Blunder. – 5. For giving information to passers-by. – 6. £10 a week.

2 1. Why – 2. Who – 3. Which – 4. How much – 5. How long – 6. What… like – 7. How far.

3 *Corrigé suggéré* : 1. Whose (surfboard) is it? – 2. How many times did you train in Biarritz this year? – 3. Who went surfing with you?

38 Les pronoms relatifs p. 49

1 1. who – 2. which – 3. whose – 4. What, what – 5. that.

2 1. My mother has a cat whose fur is grey. – 2. He lent me a book which is very interesting. – 3. I've just hired an engineer who was a teacher before. – 4. *Frankenstein* is a book which was written by Mary Shelley. – 5. I did not listen to what he said.

3 1. Mr Bell is the man who invented the telephone. – 2. The telephone which we use has changed a lot. – 3. All the people that use the telephone are satisfied. – 4. But the businessmen and women whose telephone does not work are furious.

39 Les prépositions p. 50

1 1. outside – 2. between – 3. above – 4. on the left.

2 1. At; in – 2. on; at – 3. In; on – 4. at – 5. on.

ANNEXES

Vocabulaire : bilan sous forme de jeux p. 50

1 Si vous avez trouvé 10 mots, c'est bien ; 20 mots, c'est très bien et si vous en avez trouvé 30 : vous êtes un champion !

2 1. EMBARRASSED : dear – bear – beer – mad – red – read – at – bed – be – bee – dream – dress, etc.

2. ENTHUSIASTIC : at – seat – sit – heat – has – sun – as – the – that – tea – ten – case – catch – hate, etc.

3 1. e – 2. k – 3. f – 4. c – 5. i – 6. l – 7. b – 8. h – 9. m – 10. a – 11. n – 12. d – 13. j – 14. g

4

	A	B	C	D	E	F	G	H
1	s	a	t	u	r	d	a	y
2	c			s	c	o	r	e
3	i	f		e			c	s
4	e	l		l	i	g	h	t
5	n	i	n	e		r		e
6	t	e	a	s		o		r
7	i	s		s	o	u	n	d
8	s					n		a
9	t	r	e	e		d	a	y

Corrigés détachables

© Cahier du jour/Cahier du soir – Anglais 4e

20 L'infinitif

→ Corrigés p. II

Observer et retenir

A terrific invention

MR DULL: What is this gadget for?

MR BRIGHT: **To clean** the windows.

MR DULL: What must you **do to make it work**?

MR BRIGHT: Just press this button. Can you **see** the arm **rise**?

MR DULL: Fantastic! Who ordered you **to invent** it?

MR BRIGHT: Nobody. But mother was too tired **to clean** the windows... and she was always asking me **to do** it!

MR DULL: Very clever! Let her **rest**... and let's **have** a nice cup of coffee!

■ On trouve la **base verbale** après :

- les **modaux**

Exemple *Can you **see** the arm rise?*

- ***let***

Exemple ***Let** her **have** a rest!*

- ***make*** (= faire + infinitif en français)

Exemple ***Make** it **work**.*

- les **verbes de perception**

Exemple *I **saw** mother **work** with the machine.*

■ On emploie ***to* + base verbale** :

- pour indiquer le **but**

Exemple *What for? – **To clean** the windows.*

- après les **verbes d'ordre**, **de volonté**

Exemple *I **want to clean** the windows.*

- dans la **proposition infinitive**

Exemple *She wanted me **to clean** the windows.*

S'entraîner

1 ★ Dans les phrases suivantes, utiliseriez-vous la base verbale ou *to* + base verbale ? Entourez la solution choisie.

1. I let my dog (run – to run) into my neighbour's garden.
2. Everybody in the world wants (be – to be) free.
3. I could hear the crowd (shout – to shout) in the stadium.
4. Stephen tried (get – to get) a ticket for the World Cup.
5. Supporters always want their team (win – to win).

2 ★★ Complétez les phrases suivantes avec les verbes proposés en fin de phrase. Dans toutes les phrases, utilisez une proposition infinitive.

1. Do you want Henry to stay or do you want (leave) ....?
2. Would you like your daughter to go to university or would you like (look for) .... a job immediately?
3. Do you want me to buy this novel or would you like (borrow) .... it from the library?
4. Farmers can produce a lot of milk but the government orders (limit) .... their production.

3 ★★★ Traduisez les phrases suivantes.

1. Je suis fatigué. Laissez-moi respirer un peu !

....

2. Johnny a fait jouer tous ses musiciens.

....

3. D'ici je peux entendre sonner les cloches.

....

4. Notre professeur d'anglais nous a fait lire *Robinson Crusoé*.

....

....

Auto évaluation Très bien ☐ Bien ☐ Pas assez bien ☐

*il peut être sujet ou COD

21 Le gérondif

* nom constitué d'un verbe en anglais auquel on ajoute la terminaison -ing-
* il a la même fonction qu'un nom (même s'il ressemble à un verbe)

→ Corrigés p. II

GRAMMAIRE

Observer et retenir

Likes and dislikes

ARTHUR: Are you fond of **camping**?

BETTY: I don't mind **sleeping** in the open when the weather is fine.

ARTHUR: So, what about **going** to the country tomorrow? I enjoy **running** in the woods.

BETTY: I love **jogging** but I can't bear **running** in the rain. The weather is too nasty. Why not go to the gym instead of **getting** wet in the country?

■ Le **gérondif** (base verbale + *-ing*) s'emploie :

- après **certaines prépositions** : *of, about, for, instead of...*

Exemples *... **instead of getting** wet in the country.*
*What **about going** to the country?*

- après les **verbes de sentiment** : *like, dislike, hate, love, enjoy, be fond of...*

Exemple *Are you **fond of camping**?*

- après des **expressions** telles que : *I can't stand, I can't bear, I don't mind...*

Exemple *I **don't mind sleeping** in the open.*

Attention
Certains verbes sont suivis de la **base verbale** ou de ***to* + base verbale**. (Voir la fiche 20.)

S'entraîner

1 ★ Complétez les phrases suivantes en utilisant le gérondif des verbes ci-dessous :
dance – listen to – sing – study

1. Usually teenagers enjoy .... rock singers.
2. They are fond of .... and ....
3. What about .... another language than English?

2 ★★ Choisissez la forme qui convient au verbe entre parenthèses : base verbale, *to* + base verbale ou gérondif.

1. I'd like (meet) .... my favourite singer.
2. Would you (speak) .... louder, please?
3. I can't stand (queue) .... at the supermarket cashdesks.
4. What is a computer for? (calculate) .... faster.
5. What do you want this computer for? (type) .... my exposé.

3 ★★★ Complétez les phrases suivantes à l'aide des termes ci-dessous :

after – be fond of – can't bear – 'd like – dream of – enjoy – not like

1. John .... driving. He .... to be 16.
2. He .... watching car races.
3. He .... becoming a race driver himself!
4. .... training a lot he will become a champion.
5. Of course he .... driving on roads.

Auto évaluation Très bien ☐ Bien ☐ Pas assez bien ☐

22 There is/there are

→ Corrigés p. III

Observer et retenir

Trouble in town

FATHER: What a traffic jam! **There must be** a demonstration nearby.

SON: **There is** one today, **there was** one yesterday and **there will be** one tomorrow! **There is** one every day.

FATHER: Last week **there were** dangerous hooligans in this street. **There should be** more police in this district.

SON: Look! **There has just been** an accident. It was not a demonstration.

■ ***There is*** **+ nom au singulier** et ***there are*** **+ nom au pluriel** peuvent :

- se conjuguer à tous les temps → ***There was*** *a demonstration yesterday.* ***There has just been*** *an accident.*
- se combiner avec les modaux → ***There will be*** *one tomorrow.* ***There should be*** *more police.*

■ On les utilise pour **décrire**, **renseigner**, **exprimer une opinion**.

S'entraîner

1 ★ Complétez les phrases suivantes en utilisant suivant le sens : *there will be*, *there would be*, *there was*, *there were*.

1. In the next century .... many more computers than now.
2. In the past .... a typing machine in my father's office.
3. If drivers used a better fuel .... less pollution.
4. When I was in the States .... three churches in the village I lived in.

2 ★ Transformez les phrases proposées en utilisant *there + be* ou *there + modal + be* suivant le sens des phrases.

1. My father has got a lot of books.

There .... a lot of books in my father's office.

2. His house seems to be big.

There .... a lot of rooms.

3. They are building a new restaurant here.

There .... a new restaurant here.

4. The students are too numerous in this class.

There .... another teacher.

5. My brother would like to play the guitar, but it is too noisy in a flat.

There .... too much noise in the house.

3 ★★★ Traduisez les phrases suivantes.

1. Le bus est en retard ; il doit y avoir une grève.

→ ....

2. Il y avait beaucoup d'invités au mariage.

→ ....

3. Y a-t-il des garages dans cette ville ?

→ ....

4. Y a-t-il un pilote dans l'avion ?

→ ....

5. Il y aura beaucoup de supporters dans le stade.

→ ....

6. Il devrait y avoir beaucoup d'oranges cette année.

→ ....

Auto évaluation Très bien ☐ Bien ☐ Pas assez bien ☐

23 Les propositions subordonnées de temps

→ Corrigés p. III

Observer et retenir

1. **As soon as** she **was** 25, Elizabeth I **became** Queen of England. **While** she **was** Queen, she **organised** anglicanism. **When** she **died**, James I **reigned** over England and Scotland.

2. SON: When will I drive a car?
FATHER: **As soon as** you **are** 16.
SON: When will I have the right to vote?
FATHER: **When** you **are** 18.

■ Les propositions subordonnées de temps sont **introduites par des conjonctions de temps**. (Voir aussi la fiche 11.)

	L'évènement...	Conjonctions utilisées	Verbe de la principale	Verbes de la subordonnée
1	... a eu lieu dans le passé.	*when/while* *just as* *as soon as*	*simple past*	*simple past* ou *simple past* en *-ing*
2	... aura lieu dans un futur proche ou lointain	*as soon as* *when*	futur en *will*	présent simple

Exemples *As soon as she **was** 25, Elizabeth I **became**...*
*You'**ll have** the right to vote **when** you are 18.*

■ Le **futur antérieur français** se traduit par un ***present perfect*** dans la subordonnée de temps.

Exemple *You'**ll buy** a car **when** you **have passed** your driving test.*

S'entraîner

1 ★ Complétez avec une conjonction de temps suivant le sens de la phrase. Utilisez *as soon as*, *just as*, *when*, *while*.

1. .... she was driving back home, it started raining.
2. .... she arrived home, there was a clap of thunder.
3. She thought: "......................... I arrive, I'll give Tom a call."
4. .... I have phoned him, I'll feel better.

2 ★★ Complétez avec les verbes entre parenthèses à la forme qui convient.

1. Exchanges were easier as soon as the euro (become) .... the official currency in all countries.
2. When I (complete) .... my studies, I'll work in Germany.
3. When I (be) .... younger, I couldn't imagine that Europe (exist) .... one day.
4. While I (look for) .... a job, a German businessman (offer) .... me one.

3 ★★★ Sur une feuille à part, traduisez les phrases suivantes.

1. Quand il était sur son île, Robinson Crusoé n'avait qu'un ami.
2. Pendant que Robinson chassait, Vendredi faisait la cuisine.
3. Robinson pensait : « Quand un bateau arrivera, j'allumerai un grand feu. »
4. Vendredi pensait : « Lorsque Robinson sera parti, qu'est-ce qui m'arrivera ? »

Auto évaluation Très bien ☐ Bien ☐ Pas assez bien ☐

24 Le passif

→ Corrigés p. III

Observer et retenir

A headmaster to a student

When you arrived in our school, you **were given** some responsibilities. Up to now you **have been considered** as a very good student. Some of your teachers thought you **should be oriented** towards a famous university. And I am sure their decision **will be approved of** by all your mates. So I wish you good luck.

Formation du passif : *be* + participe passé

Ordre des mots dans la phrase

Sujet	+	(modal)	+	*be*	+	participe passé	+	(complément d'agent)
You		(Ø)		*are*		*considered as a very good student*		*(by all your teachers)*
You		*should*		*be*		*oriented towards a famous university*		(Ø)

Emploi

- Le passif insiste sur ce qui arrive au sujet, animé ou inanimé.
- Le complément d'agent n'apparaît que lorsqu'il apporte une précision nécessaire.

Exemple *This decision will be approved of **by all your mates**.*

S'entraîner

1 ★ Mettez les phrases suivantes à la voix passive.

1. The Head sent this student to university.

→ ....

2. The Head has written a letter to recommend her.

→ ....

3. Her new mates will welcome her heartily.

→ ....

4. I'm sure her new teachers will appreciate her work.

→ ....

2 ★★ Complétez les phrases suivantes avec un groupe verbal à la voix passive en utilisant le verbe et la forme indiqués entre parenthèses.

1. John (just hire/present perfect) .... as a journalist.

2. He (immediately send/simple past) .... to Italy last week.

3. When in Rome, he (help/future) .... by a colleague.

4. His articles (write/must) .... in Italian.

5. Such a job (consider/can) .... as an exciting one.

3 ★★★ Traduisez en utilisant la voix passive.

1. On est invités samedi prochain.

→ ....

2. On nous attendra à la porte.

→ ....

3. Des boissons fraîches seront servies.

→ ....

4. On a envoyé cette invitation à cent personnes.

→ ....

5. Ils seront bien accueillis.

→ ....

6. Sa voiture a été volée.

→ ....

Auto évaluation Très bien ☐ Bien ☐ Pas assez bien ☐

25 So/neither

→ Corrigés p. III

Observer et retenir

Man's best friend

FRED: You've invited him, **haven't you**?

TONY: Yes, **I have**.

FRED: You don't like him very much, **do you**?

TONY: No, **I don't**. He's got too loud a voice, **hasn't he**?

FRED: Yes, **he has**. And I don't like his mouth.

TONY: **Neither do I**. But I like his green eyes.

FRED: **So do I**.

ARTHUR: Who are you talking about?

FRED: Tony's dog, of course!

Réponses brèves

On reprend l'auxiliaire (ou le modal) de la question dans la réponse.

Exemple – *You've invited him,* ***haven't you****?*
– *Yes, I have.*

Recherche d'approbation (*question tags*)

- Après une proposition négative, dans la seconde partie de la phrase, auxiliaire (ou modal) + sujet

Exemple *You don't like him,* ***do you****?*

- Après une proposition positive, auxiliaire (ou modal) + *not* + sujet

Exemple *You've invited him,* ***haven't you****?*

Approbation positive (aussi)

So + auxiliaire (ou modal) + sujet

Exemple – *I like his green eyes.*
– ***So do I.***

Approbation négative (non plus)

Neither + auxiliaire (ou modal) + sujet

Exemple – *I don't like his mouth.*
– ***Neither do I.***

S'entraîner

1 ★ Complétez les phrases avec des *question tags*.

1. You like modern painting, ... ?
2. He hasn't seen him for months, ... ?
3. Your parents never allow you to travel alone, ... ?
4. You can phone her to come, ... ?
5. Your sister will go to the States, ... ?

2 ★★ Suivant le sens de la phrase, réagissez positivement ou négativement. Utilisez comme sujet les mots donnés à la fin de chaque ligne.

1. Tony has got a dog.
→ .... (Arthur)
2. I can't stand crowded buses.
→ .... (My mother)
3. Gene loved dancing.
→ .... (Fred)
4. Everybody will be ready at 12.
→ .... (I)
5. I have never seen such a match.
→ .... (I)

3 ★★★ Inventez des phrases qui pourraient se terminer par les *question tags* suivants.

1. ...., weren't they?
2. ...., hadn't they?
3. ...., didn't they?
4. ...., can they?

Auto évaluation Très bien ☐ Bien ☐ Pas assez bien ☐

26 Some/any

→ Corrigés p. III

Observer et retenir

In the old castle

PETER: Knock, knock! Is there **anybody** in here?

JEAN: Let's come in and see.

PETER: Look! A fridge. Is there **any** water or milk left?

JEAN: No. There is **some** bread. **Some of** it has already been eaten by mice.

PETER: If you find **any** drink, just tell me. I'm thirsty.

JEAN: We **don't** have **any** time to look for that. We have **nothing** to do here. Let's go out.

Emploi

- Dans une **affirmation** : *some* (et composés)
- Dans une **négation** : *any* (et composés)

Exemple *We don't have **any** time.*

- Dans une **interrogation** : *any* (et composés)

Exemple *Is there **anybody** in here?*

- **Après *if*** : *any* (et composés)

Exemple *If you find **any drink**...*

Some et *any* indiquent une **quantité non précisée**.

Exemple *some bread, some drink.*

Remarques

- *Some of*, *any of* s'emploient pour indiquer une **partie non déterminée d'un ensemble**.
Ex. : ***Some of the bread*** *has been eaten by mice.*
- *Some*, *any* et *no* peuvent **se combiner** avec : *-one, -body, -thing, -where.*
- *No* et ses composés peuvent s'employer dans une **phrase négative**.
Ex. : *We have **nothing** to do.*

S'entraîner

1 ★ Reliez les éléments des deux colonnes afin de composer des phrases.

1. I wonder if... •
2. I don't know... •
3. Is there... •
4. I'm sure... •

- • a. ... nobody is interested.
- • b. ... there is anything good on TV tonight.
- • c. ... anything about the programmes.
- • d. ... anybody to watch the thriller with me?

2 ★★ Complétez les phrases suivantes à l'aide de *some*, *any*, *no* et de leurs composés.

1. Peter and Mary knocked at the door, but .... came.
2. They tried to find if there was .... milk left.
3. But they couldn't find ....
4. Did they have .... chance to find ....?
5. In fact there wasn't .... nor .... in that castle.

3 ★★★ Sur une feuille à part, traduisez les phrases suivantes.

1. Mary pensait qu'elle trouverait quelqu'un à qui parler.
2. Mais elle n'a pu voir personne.
3. Elle avait quelque chose d'important à dire.
4. De toute façon elle parlerait à n'importe qui, quelque part, n'importe où.

Auto évaluation Très bien ☐ Bien ☐ Pas assez bien ☐

27 L'article (cas général)

→ Corrigés p. III

Observer et retenir

The queen

PAUL: Hurrah! I've never seen **a** queen in my life!
BEN: **A** queen? Which queen?
PAUL: **The** Queen of England, Ø Queen Elizabeth.

A lama

JUNIOR: Look, Granny, **a** lama. Where does it live?
GRANNY: It lives in Ø nature, in **the** Andes.
JUNIOR: Oh, Granny, **the** lama is coming near.
GRANNY: Ø Lamas are not dangerous. But mind! They spit!

■ Un **nom** peut être plus ou moins **déterminé**.

Ø → *A, An* → *Some* → *The*

- **absence de détermination** → *Ø Lamas are not dangerous.*
- **détermination faible (au singulier)** → *Look, Granny, a lama.*
- **détermination faible (au pluriel)** → *There are **some** lamas in this zoo.*
- **détermination forte** → ***The** lama is coming near.*

Remarque

N'importe quel **nom** peut être **déterminé par** un **complément**, une **proposition** ou le **contexte**. Dans ce cas, on emploie l'article *the*.

Ex. : *The lamas of this zoo are well-fed. The lama I saw in the zoo yesterday was asleep.*

Ex. : *Daddy, I saw a lama yesterday; the lama spat at me.*

S'entraîner

1 ★ Complétez les phrases avec : Ø, a (ou *an*), *some*, *the*.

1. .... Ireland is .... green country.
2. .... Irishmen drink too much beer but most of them don't.
3. There is .... pub in each Irish village.
4. .... Irish grow .... potatoes and breed .... cattle.
5. .... Irishmen still emigrate to .... States.

2 ★★ Entourez la réponse qui convient pour compléter les phrases suivantes.

1. (A teenager – The teenagers – Teenagers) are fond of sports.
2. (A teenager – The teenagers – Teenagers) of the 21st century will enjoy virtual reality.
3. (A teenager – The teenagers – Teenagers) I met in the Netherlands were all bilingual.
4. (Some teenagers – The teenagers – Teenagers) play football, others prefer watching matches.
5. At Ashford School (some teenagers – the teenagers – teenagers) wear uniforms.

3 ★★★ Sur une feuille à part, traduisez les phrases suivantes.

1. J'ai visité un pays, le pays dont je rêvais.
2. Les femmes de ce pays portent des jupes longues.
3. Là-bas, j'ai vu des animaux étranges.
4. L'animal le plus extraordinaire avait deux têtes.
5. Il y avait des serpents qui sortaient de sa gueule.

Auto évaluation Très bien ☐ Bien ☐ Pas assez bien ☐

28 L'article (cas particuliers)

→ Corrigés p. III

Observer et retenir

– **The** United Kingdom is made of Ø Great Britain and Ø Northern Ireland.
– **The** Queen reigns but **the** Prime Minister governs **the** country.
– Ø Britain produces Ø coal, Ø wool and Ø hi-tech materials.
– **The** English like betting on Ø football matches and Ø horse races.
– "I have nothing to offer but Ø blood, Ø tears and Ø sweat," Churchill said during Ø World War II.

Absence d'article
– noms de personnes au singulier (**ex. :** *John Smith*)
– noms abstraits (**ex. :** *The Red Badge of Courage*)
– noms de lieux au singulier (**ex. :** *At school, France, Oxford St*)
– aliments et repas (**ex. :** *Milk for breakfast*)
– matières et matériaux (**ex. :** *Chocolate is kept in silver paper.*)
– jeux et sports (**ex. :** *I prefer Scrabble to rugby.*)

Présence de *the*
– noms de personnes au pluriel (**ex. :** *The Smiths*)
– chose unique (**ex. :** *The sun, the sky, the country, the sea*)
– noms de fleuves, de chaînes de montagnes, de mers (**ex. :** *The Thames, the Alps, the Indian Ocean*)
– noms de pays au pluriel (**ex. :** *The Netherlands, the USA*)
– les instruments de musique (**ex. :** *She plays the piano, not the violin.*)

S'entraîner

1 ★ Trouvez dans le texte en haut de page un/ou plusieurs noms correspondant aux catégories suivantes.

1. Nom de pays : ....
2. Titre : ....
3. Nom de matière : ....
4. Sport : ....

2 ★★ Complétez les phrases suivantes avec Ø ou *the*.

1. Winston Churchill spoke .... language of .... courage.
2. He loved .... painting and smoking .... cigars.
3. He lived in .... Kent and worked on .... Downing Street.
4. To meet .... President Roosevelt, he went by .... boat to .... middle of .... Atlantic Ocean.
5. When he was at .... school, he didn't like .... Greek.

3 ★★★ Sur une feuille à part, traduisez les phrases suivantes.

1. Les Alpes s'étendent de la France à l'Autriche.
2. Le ciel est clair ; on peut voir le mont Blanc.
3. Dans ce film, elle jouait du piano sur la plage.
4. Certains aiment aller au bord de la mer, d'autres à la montagne.
5. La tour Eiffel est la tour la plus haute de Paris.

Auto évaluation — Très bien ☐ Bien ☐ Pas assez bien ☐

GRAMMAIRE

29 Dénombrables et indénombrables

→ Corrigés p. III

Observer et retenir

(1) – There is a lot of **traffic** today.

(2) – Look! there's **a traffic jam** ahead.

(3) – Have you got a lot of **luggage**?

(4) – No, just **a case** and **a bag**.

(5) – What horrible **weather**! It won't be **a nice day**.

(6) – I don't know where to put all my **furniture**, twelve chairs; two tables… There isn't enough **room**.

(7) – People always say: "The **news** is bad today."

Dénombrable :

– que l'on peut compter ;
– prend la marque du pluriel.

Remarques

- Certains noms appartiennent aux deux catégories avec deux sens différents.
Time is money. (*time* = temps)
Have a good time! (*time* = moment)
- *People* et *the police* sont suivis d'un verbe au pluriel.

Indénombrable :

– que l'on ne peut pas compter ;
– ne prend pas la marque du pluriel ;
– ne peut être précédé d'un article indéfini.

Exemples

– noms de matière : *milk, bread,* etc.
– noms abstraits : *luck, work,* etc.
– certains noms représentant des ensembles : *information, luggage, furniture, traffic, weather, damage, money,* etc.

S'entraîner

1 ★ Classez en trois catégories les mots suivants dans le tableau.

banana – bread – business – information – job – key – music – mutton – noise – room

dénombrables	indénombrables	dénombrables ou indénombrables

2 ★★ Complétez les phrases avec les verbes indiqués à la 3e personne du singulier ou du pluriel.

1. My luggage (be) .... very heavy today.
2. Information (be).................... given at the desk near by.
3. In England people (be) .... always ready to help.
4. The police (have) .... just arrested the gangster.

3 ★★ Complétez les phrases avec *a*, *an* ou Ø.

1. A lot of unemployed people are looking for .... job.
2. To get informed I buy .... paper every day.
3. Did you have .... fun at Betty's party?
4. In my family, we always eat .... mutton for Easter.

4 ★★★ Traduisez les phrases suivantes.

1. Ma voisine a les cheveux longs.

→ ....

2. Je n'ai pas de chance mais j'ai du courage.

→ ....

3. Quelles sont les nouvelles ? Achète-moi un journal, s'il te plaît.

→ ....

Auto évaluation Très bien ☐ Bien ☐ Pas assez bien ☐

30 Les quantificateurs

→ Corrigés p. III

Observer et retenir

Shopping

MR SMITH: **Some** butter, please.

MILKMAN: **How much** do you want?

MR SMITH: **A little**. Stop! I didn't tell you **a lot of** butter. You are giving me **too much**.

When I went shopping, I didn't know **how many** oranges to buy: three or four perhaps… well, **a few**, not **a lot**. When I buy **too many**, they get spoilt. Three will be **enough**.

■ Les quantificateurs suivants **précèdent un nom**.

Dénombrable	Indénombrable
how many	*how much*
some	*some*
a few	*a little*
a lot of	*a lot of*
(many)	*(much)*
too many	*too much*

Remarques

- ***Enough*** s'emploie devant un dénombrable ou un indénombrable.
- ***Much*** et ***many*** s'emploient dans les phrases négatives ou interrogatives.

S'entraîner

1 ★ Les phrases des deux colonnes se complètent. Reliez-les suivant le sens.

1. I don't want too much. •
2. There aren't many people today. •
3. Take a taxi! •
4. I won't take my car today. •
5. This house is very expensive. •
6. You were very helpful. •

- • a. There is too much traffic.
- • b. A lot of thanks.
- • c. Just a few.
- • d. You don't have enough time.
- • e. Give me a little cheese.
- • f. She is rich. She can buy it.

2 ★★ Complétez avec le quantificateur qui convient.

1. This flat is too small; there isn't .... room.
2. I haven't got .... money, just .... coins.
3. I can't work in this class; there is .... noise.
4. Mary is really sick; she's eaten .... cakes.
5. He doesn't read ....; there are only .... books in his house.

3 ★★★ Remettez les mots dans l'ordre.

1. a – few – have – hours – I – spend – to – with – you

→ ....

2. are – football – many – matches – on – television – there – too

→ ....

3. a – but – did – efforts – he – he – lot – made – make – much – of – progress – not

→ ....

4. a – a – better – is – kindness – little – lot – money – of – than

→ ....

Auto évaluation Très bien ☐ Bien ☐ Pas assez bien ☐

31 Le génitif

→ Corrigés p. III

Observer et retenir

A busy old man

Though he is quite old, he likes taking **an hour's walk** every day. Either he goes to **Susan's** (Susan is his sister) or to the **butcher's**. Sometimes he stops at **the Browns'**. He likes talking with his **neighbours'** children. When back home, he has a look at **the door of the garage** and invariably thinks: "Why didn't I take my car… or my **wife's**?"

Règle générale

- Le génitif met en relation un « possesseur » (être animé) et une chose possédée (inanimée).
- La marque du génitif est :

– **'s** après un nom singulier ou un pluriel en *-en*

– **'** après un nom pluriel

Ellipse

- On peut omettre les mots *house, shop, church* après la marque du génitif.

Exemples *He goes to Susan**'s** (house).*

*My car… or my wife**'s** (car).*

Remarques

- On peut employer le génitif dans les expressions de mesure.

Ex. : *an hour's walk; a two miles' walk*

- Quand on assemble deux noms de choses, on utilise généralement la construction avec *of* ou un nom composé.

Ex. : *the door of the garage; the garage door.*

S'entraîner

1 ★★ **Réunissez les deux mots qui vous sont proposés soit avec un génitif, soit avec la construction en *of*.**

Attention

Il est parfois nécessaire d'ajouter des articles.

1. back/room → ....
2. book/Peter → ....
3. car/the Browns → ....
4. office/boss → ....
5. leg/table → ....
6. brush/painter → ....
7. joys/life → ....
8. top/mountain → ....
9. gate/traitor → ....
10. talk/three minutes → ....

2 ★★ **Sur une feuille à part, reformulez les phrases suivantes en formant un génitif avec les mots soulignés.**

1. Last week I was at <u>the wedding of Charles and Mary</u>.
2. <u>The job of a bus driver</u> is tiring.
3. <u>The shop of the butcher</u> is near <u>the house of the Smiths</u>.
4. The President gave <u>a speech of two hours</u>.

3 ★★★ **Imaginez des réponses aux questions suivantes.**

1. Whose house is this?

→ It's ....

2. Whose bicycles are those?

→ They are ....

3. Whose boat is this?

→ It's ....

Auto évaluation Très bien ☐ Bien ☐ Pas assez bien ☐

32 Les noms composés

→ Corrigés p. III

Observer et retenir

A depressing day

As usual, Tony had **money problems**. He was walking up and down in his **sitting room** and thinking: "The **income tax** to pay, my **car accident**, and my **insurance company**, and my **health problems**… What's his **phone number**?" He meant the **bank manager's** phone number. But it was a **bank holiday**. The manager was probably at the **swimming-pool** or playing **table tennis** or watching a good **TV programme**. Poor Tony! All by himself with a **headache**, a **stomach ache**… He took a **sleeping pill** and slept all over the **weekend**.

■ Les noms composés se forment en **juxtaposant deux noms.** Le **premier nom caractérise le second,** un peu comme un adjectif.

Exemple *money problems* (des problèmes d'argent)

■ L'ordre des mots est le plus souvent à l'inverse du français.

■ Les noms composés s'**écrivent**, suivant l'usage :
– soit en **un mot** (*weekend*) ;
– soit en **deux mots** réunis par un **trait d'union** (*dining-table*) ;
– soit en **deux mots** (*table tennis*).

S'entraîner

1 ★ Trouvez les noms composés qui correspondent aux définitions suivantes, à l'aide des mots soulignés.

1. Une machine à laver. ……………………………
2. Un sac pour faire des courses. ……………………………
3. Un verre à vin. ……………………………
4. Une boutique où l'on vend des livres. ……………………………
5. Un journal qui paraît le matin. ……………………………

2 ★★ Après avoir relu le texte en haut de la page, trouvez les noms composés qui complètent les phrases.

1. When you take aspirin, it is because you have a ……………………………
2. If you go to the doctor's, it is because you have ……………………………
3. At the head of a bank there is a ……………………………
4. In England banks are closed on ……………………………
5. Every year you have to pay your …………………………… to the state.
6. When you want to call a friend, you dial his ……………………………
7. A car accident? Just phone your ……………………………

3 ★★★ Sur une feuille à part, traduisez les phrases suivantes en utilisant des noms composés, à l'aide des mots soulignés.

1. Les vacances d'été sont plus longues que les vacances de Pâques.
2. La porte du garage est ouverte ; l'autoradio a été volé.
3. Que préférez-vous, les romans d'amour ou les romans policiers ?
4. Rentrerez-vous par le train du soir ou par le vol de nuit ?

Auto évaluation Très bien ☐ Bien ☐ Pas assez bien ☐

33 L'exclamation

→ Corrigés p. III

Observer et retenir

Summer stars

MR BLUE: **What a** boring evening!
MR BLACK: Oh, yes! He told us **such a** long story.
MR BLUE: The stories he tells are always **so** long.
MR BLACK: Let's forget him! Look! **What** splendid stars! **How** beautiful they are!
MR BLUE: You can only see **such** beautiful stars in August.
MR BLACK: Stars are always **so** beautiful to watch… when there are no clouds!

■ **Composition**

Dénombrables		Indénombrables
What a + singulier	***What*** + pluriel	***What***
What a boring evening!	*What splendid stars!*	*What nice weather!*
Such a + singulier	***Such*** + pluriel	***Such***
Such a long story!	*Such long stories!*	*They had such fun!*

Remarque
What a shame! (Quelle honte !)
What a pity! (Quel dommage !)

■ ***How*** et ***so*** précèdent un adjectif ou un adverbe :

Exemples ***How*** *nice she is!*
She is ***so*** *nice.*

S'entraîner

1 ★ Reformulez les phrases exclamatives suivantes en remplaçant *what (a)* par *such (a)* ou vice versa.

1. What nice weather we had!
→ ……………………………………………………………
2. He is such an unpleasant person!
→ ……………………………………………………………
3. Tony had such fun at the funfair!
→ ……………………………………………………………
4. What a beautiful car you bought!
→ ……………………………………………………………

2 ★ Complétez avec *so*, *such* ou *such a*.

1. They made …………… noise that I couldn't sleep.
2. This actress is ………………………… fascinating that everybody loves her.
3. She is ………………………… fascinating actress that she plays in a lot of films.
4. They had ……………… work that they couldn't go on holiday.

3 ★★ Entourez le mot exclamatif qui convient.

1. (How – What a – Such) lovely the garden was!
2. (How – What a – Such) splendid cathedral!
3. (How – What a – Such) courage must be rewarded.
4. They have never had (how – what a – such a) pleasant journey.

4 ★★★ Sur une feuille à part, traduisez les phrases suivantes.

1. Quel brillant élève !
2. Quel horrible temps nous avons eu la semaine dernière !
3. Je n'ai jamais rencontré une personne aussi intéressante.
4. Il est si heureux qu'il chante tout le temps.

Auto évaluation Très bien ☐ Bien ☐ Pas assez bien ☐

34 Comparatif et superlatif

→ Corrigés p. IV

Observer et retenir

Knowing more

DAUGHTER: Daddy, is the Thames **longer than** the Seine?

FATHER: I suppose it is.

DAUGHTER: Daddy, what's **the longest** river in England?

FATHER: Look up in the dictionary.

DAUGHTER: Daddy, what is **the most powerful** animal?

FATHER: The elephant… or the whale.

DAUGHTER: Daddy, is the elephant **more powerful than** the whale?

FATHER: I can't tell… Let's say… the elephant is **as powerful as** the whale… but perhaps it is **not as powerful**.

DAUGHTER: Oh, Daddy, you don't know anything. I'll ask Mummy.

	Adjectifs d'une syllabe	Adjectifs de deux syllabes en *-y*	Adjectifs de deux syllabes ou plus
Comparatif d'égalité	***as*** + adjectif + ***as***	***as*** + adjectif + ***as***	***as*** + adjectif + ***as***
Comparatif de supériorité	adjectif ***-er*** + ***than***	adjectif ***-ier*** + ***than***	***more*** + adjectif + ***than***
Comparatif d'inégalité	***not as*** + adjectif + ***as***	***not as*** + adjectif + ***as***	***not as*** + adjectif + ***as***
Comparatif d'infériorité	***less*** + adjectif + ***than***	***less*** + adjectif + ***than***	***less*** + adjectif + ***than***
Superlatif de supériorité	***the*** + adjectif ***-est***	***the*** + adjectif ***-iest***	***the most*** + adjectif

Attention
Il y a des **exceptions** :
good → *better* → *the best.*

S'entraîner

1 ★ Complétez les phrases avec *expensive*, *good* ou *warm* au comparatif de supériorité.

1. This room is very cold. Can we go to a .... place?
2. This camera is quite cheap. I thought it was ....
3. You don't know your lesson. I'm sure you can do .. ..

2 ★★ Complétez les phrases avec le type de comparatif indiqué ainsi que l'adjectif proposé.

1. **Égalité** → Paul is (intelligent) .... Thomas.
2. **Supériorité** → A kilo of iron is not (heavy) .... a kilo of feathers.
3. **Infériorité** → A cold is (serious) .... the flu.
4. **Supériorité** → Buses are (crowded) .... at 6 p.m. .... at 10 a.m.

3 ★★★ Complétez en utilisant le comparatif ou le superlatif des adjectifs indiqués.

1. The plane is certainly (fast) .... means of transport.
2. In 2003, *Harry Potter* was (successful) .... film of the year.
3. A tiger is (dangerous) .... a cat.
4. Sumotoris are (fat) .... men in the world.
5. Water is (necessary) .... to man .... air.

Auto évaluation Très bien ☐ Bien ☐ Pas assez bien ☐

35 Les adjectifs composés

→ Corrigés p. IV

Observer et retenir

At the restaurant

This is a great restaurant! It's such a **nice-looking** place. They serve delicious food. I love their **strawberry-flavoured** cake. It's **house-made**!

- Un **adjectif composé** comporte **deux éléments**. Le **premier** élément apporte une **précision**.
- Un adjectif composé se comporte comme un adjectif ! Il est **invariable** et **se place avant le nom** lorsqu'il est **épithète**.
- **Composition**
  - adjectif + adjectif → *light green*
  - adjectif + nom verbal → *nice-looking*
  - nom + nom + *-ed* → *strawberry-flavoured*
  - nom + participe passé → *house-made*
  - nom + adjectif (en un seul mot) → *seasick*

S'entraîner

1 ★ Reliez les mots des trois colonnes en faisant attention au sens. Reportez les résultats dans la grille.

1. qui dure longtemps
2. bleu clair
3. qui court vite
4. de mauvaise humeur

a. fast-running
b. long-lasting
c. light blue
d. bad-tempered

A. speech
B. policeman
C. animal
D. dress

1	2	3	4

2 ★★★ Pour récrire ces phrases, utilisez un adjectif composé suivant les indications données. Servez-vous des mots soulignés.

1. The hare runs fast. (*adjectif + nom verbal*)

The hare is a .... animal.

2. The giant's shoulders were very broad. (*adjectif + nom + -ed*)

The giant was a .... man.

3. I wanted a blue dress, but not dark, rather light. (*adjectif + adjectif*)

I wanted a ....

4. Nowadays cars are produced in mass. (*nom + participe passé*)

Nowadays cars are ....

3 ★★★ Complétez les adjectifs avec les suffixes *-ed* ou *-ing* quand c'est nécessaire. Sinon, inscrivez le signe Ø.

1. A rabbit is a long-ear.............. animal.
2. He never listens. He is always absent-mind.............. .
3. There is no end to this story.

It is a never-end........... story.

4. A snake has a thick skin. It is a thick-skin.............. animal.
5. Give me some water, as cold as ice.

Yes, ice-cold.............. water.

6. She'll call her friend in Australia.

It is a long-distance.............. call.

Auto évaluation Très bien ☐ Bien ☐ Pas assez bien ☐

36 Les adverbes

→ Corrigés p. IV

Observer et retenir

Travelling

LILY: Are you in New York **yet**?

JAMES: No, I'm in London. I'm **still** waiting for my flight.

LILY: You've **never** been to New York, have you?

JAMES: You're right, I haven't.

LILY: It's a **really** beautiful city. I went there on holiday five years **ago**.

JAMES: It is but the flight is **rather long**. I hope I won't get too bored!

LILY: I'm sure you won't!

■ Beaucoup d'adverbes se forment en ajoutant le **suffixe *-ly*** à un adjectif. (*real* → ***really***)

■ Les adverbes se répartissent en quatre catégories principales.
- **temps** et **fréquence** : *always, never, often, sometimes, still, ago, not... yet, now*, etc. ;
- **intensification** : *much, quite, too, totally, very*, etc. ;
- **restriction** : *nearly, rather*, etc. ;
- **appréciation** : *right (You're right, right now), really*, etc.

■ **Place de l'adverbe**
- adverbes de fréquence : **devant le verbe** porteur de sens (sauf *be*) → *I'm still waiting for my flight.*
- autres adverbes : généralement **devant le mot** qu'ils modifient → *It's really beautiful.*

S'entraîner

1 ★ Remettez les mots dans l'ordre.

1. car – I – in – my – often – park – street – this

→ ....

2. almost – is – it – o'clock – ten

→ ....

3. any – can't – children – is – longer – over – play – summer – when

→ ....

2 ★★ Complétez les phrases suivantes avec l'adverbe qui convient suivant le sens de la phrase. (Tous les adverbes doivent être utilisés.) *just – quite – rather – sometimes – still – totally – very*

1. I .... agree with you. You're .... right.

2. He is a .... serious student; he works day and night.

3. Peter is .... lazy, but he .... works.

4. .... a minute! She .... has to make up.

3 ★★★ Sur une feuille à part, traduisez les phrases suivantes.

1. Elle marche toujours lentement.
2. Il choisit soigneusement ses légumes.
3. Elle n'est jamais allée en Angleterre. Pourtant elle parle bien anglais.
4. Ils pensent souvent que l'anglais est beaucoup plus utile.

Auto évaluation Très bien ☐ Bien ☐ Pas assez bien ☐

37 Les mots interrogatifs

→ Corrigés p. IV

Observer et retenir

The machine goes wrong

PASSER-BY: **How** old are you?
MACHINE: Ten miles from here.
PASSER-BY: **Where** are you from?
MACHINE: Two.
PASSER-BY: **How long** have you been working?
MACHINE: When I was young.
PASSER-BY: **Who** is your owner?
MACHINE: For two years.
PASSER-BY: **What** are you here **for**?
MACHINE: Mr Blunder.
PASSER-BY: **How much** are you paid?
MACHINE: For giving information to passers-by.
PASSER-BY: Goodbye.
MACHINE: £10 a week.
PASSER-BY: It all goes wrong. **Whose** machine is it? I must find him… or her.

■ Vous connaissez déjà bien *who, what, where, when, why, how much/many, whose.*

Mais il y a aussi :

- ***Which*** (choix) → *Here's the programme.* ***Which*** *film do you want to see?*
- ***How often*** (habitude) → ***How often*** *do you go to the States every year?*
- ***How many times*** (nombre de fois) → ***How many times*** *did you go to the States last year?*
- ***What is … like?*** (description) → ***What is*** *Mr Blunder* ***like****? – He is tall and fair-haired.*
- ***What is … for?*** (utilité) → ***What is*** *this machine* ***for****? – For giving information.*

S'entraîner

1 ★ La machine est réparée ! Écrivez les réponses correspondant aux questions du sketch ci-dessus.

1. How old […]? ……………………………………
2. Where […] from? ……………………………………
3. How long […]? ……………………………………
4. Who […]? ……………………………………
5. What […] for? ……………………………………
6. How much […]? ……………………………………

2 ★★ Complétez les phrases suivantes avec des mots interrogatifs pris dans la liste ci-dessous :
how far – how long – how much – how often – what – which – who – why

1. ……………………… did you decide to go to Hawaii? – Because it's a paradise for surfers.
2. ……………………… did you fly there with? – With my best friend, Charlie.
3. ……………………… airline did you choose? – Delta Air Lines, of course.
4. ……………………… did you pay? – $1,000.
5. ……………………… did you stay there? – Just a week.
6. ……………………… was the hotel ……………………… ? – Terrific.
7. ……………………… was the hotel from the beach? – A few minutes' ride.

3 ★★★ Trouvez les questions correspondant aux mots soulignés.

1. It's <u>Bob's</u> (surfboard).
→ ……………………………………………………
2. <u>Only four times</u>.
→ ……………………………………………………
3. <u>Bob</u> did, I told you.
→ ……………………………………………………

Auto évaluation Très bien ☐ Bien ☐ Pas assez bien ☐

38 Les pronoms relatifs

→ Corrigés p. IV

Observer et retenir

A super TV set

CUSTOMER: Good morning. **What** I need is a good TV set. I mean a TV set **that** never breaks down.

ASSISTANT: Certainly, sir.

CUSTOMER: Mr Pearson, **whose** shop is at the corner of the street, told me you were the man **who** could sell me such a TV set.

ASSISTANT: He was right. Why not have a look at the TV set **which** is in the shop window?

CUSTOMER: Oh, no. I don't want to buy a TV set **that** is second-hand… except if it is a special offer.

Antécédent	Pronom relatif
Personne, animal familier (sujet)	***Who*** ou ***that***
Personne, animal familier (objet)	***That***
Chose, idée	***Which*** ou ***that***
Appartenance, possession (personne, animal ou chose)	***Whose***

■ *What* = ce que → *You never listen to **what** I say.*

■ *That* s'emploie :

– après un superlatif → *The best **that** I have ever seen.*

– après *all* → *This parrot repeats all **that** I say.*

■ *Whose* n'est **jamais** suivi d'un **article**.

S'entraîner

1 ★ Complétez avec le pronom relatif qui convient.

1. An architect is someone .... draws plans.
2. Give me an idea .... I could develop.
3. Ask Mr Jones .... house he built.
4. .... she built is not .... I'd choose.
5. All .... I want is a house, not a palace.

2 ★★ Avec l'aide d'un pronom relatif, reliez les deux phrases afin de n'en faire qu'une.

1. My mother has a cat. Her fur is grey.

→ ....

2. He lent me a book. It is very interesting.

→ ....

3. I've just hired an engineer. She was a teacher before.

→ ....

4. *Frankenstein* is a book. It was written by Mary Shelley.

→ ....

5. I did not listen. He said something.

→ ....

3 ★★★ Traduisez les phrases suivantes en utilisant des pronoms relatifs.

1. M. Bell est l'homme qui inventa le téléphone.

→ ....

2. Le téléphone que nous utilisons a beaucoup changé.

→ ....

....

3. Toutes les personnes qui utilisent le téléphone sont satisfaites.

→ ....

....

4. Mais les hommes et les femmes d'affaires dont le téléphone ne fonctionne pas sont furieux.

→ ....

....

Auto évaluation Très bien ☐ Bien ☐ Pas assez bien ☐

39 Les prépositions

→ Corrigés p. IV

Observer et retenir

Street life

1 Man 1 is **in front of** the cinema.

2 Man 2 stands **across** the street, **opposite** the cinema.

3 Man 1 is with his dog; his dog is **near** him.

4 The boy is running **round** the corner to go **to** his friend's; his friend lives **round** the corner.

5 The cinema is **behind** the man with his dog.

6 **In** the foreground we can see a car.

7 **In** the background a van is approaching the crossroads.

8 A cyclist is right **in the middle of** the crossroads; she is riding **up** the street.

9 A beggar is sitting **against** the wall.

■ Toutes les prépositions en caractères gras sont des **prépositions de lieu**.

Rappel

Vous connaissez déjà des prépositions de temps telles que *from 6 to 8, ten to twelve, a quarter past two, before lunch, after midday…* mais aussi *during*, *for* et *since*. (Voir la fiche 13.)

S'entraîner

1 ★ Après avoir regardé l'image, complétez les phrases avec l'une des deux prépositions proposées.

1. Man 1 is (inside/outside) .... the cinema.
2. The cyclist is (behind/between) .... man 2 and the van.
3. The cinema sign is (above/under) .... man 1.
4. Man 2 is (on the left of/on the right of) .... the picture.

2 ★★ Complétez les phrases avec l'une de ces prépositions : *at*, *in*, *on*.

1. .... 7 o'clock .... the morning, Paul gets up.
2. But .... Sundays, he wakes up later, ... 10.
3. .... August, he is .... holiday.
4. Every day .... midday, he has lunch at school.
5. He was born .... the sixth of July.

Auto évaluation Très bien ☐ Bien ☐ Pas assez bien ☐

Verbes irréguliers

Base verbale	Prétérit	Participe passé	Sens usuel
be	was/were	been	être
beat	beat	beaten	battre
become	became	become	devenir
begin	began	begun	commencer
blow	blew	blown	souffler
break	broke	broken	casser
bring	brought	brought	apporter/amener
build	built	built	construire
burn	burnt	burnt	brûler
burst	burst	burst	éclater
buy	bought	bought	acheter
catch	caught	caught	attraper
choose	chose	chosen	choisir
come	came	come	venir
cost	cost	cost	coûter
cut	cut	cut	couper
do	did	done	faire
draw	drew	drawn	dessiner
drink	drank	drunk	boire
drive	drove	driven	conduire
eat	ate	eaten	manger
fall	fell	fallen	tomber
feed	fed	fed	nourrir
feel	felt	felt	sentir
fight	fought	fought	battre
find	found	found	trouver
fly	flew	flown	voler
forget	forgot	forgotten	oublier
freeze	froze	frozen	geler
get	got	got	obtenir
give	gave	given	donner
go	went	gone	aller
grow	grew	grown	pousser/faire pousser/grandir
hang	hung	hung	suspendre/pendre
have	had	had	avoir
hear	heard	heard	entendre
hide	hid	hidden	(se) cacher
hit	hit	hit	frapper
hold	held	held	tenir
hurt	hurt	hurt	faire mal
keep	kept	kept	garder
know	knew	known	savoir
lead	led	led	mener
leave	left	left	laisser
lend	lent	lent	prêter
lie	lay	lain	être étendu
lose	lost	lost	perdre

make	made	made	faire
mean	meant	meant	vouloir dire
meet	met	met	rencontrer
mow	mowed	mown	tondre
pay	paid	paid	payer
put	put	put	mettre
read	read	read	lire
rent	rent	rent	louer
ride	rode	ridden	aller à vélo
ring	rang	rung	sonner
run	ran	run	courir
say	said	said	dire
see	saw	seen	voir
sell	sold	sold	vendre
send	sent	sent	envoyer
set	set	set	poser, placer
shake	shook	shaken	secouer
shine	shone	shone	briller
shoot	shot	shot	tirer (arme à feu)
show	showed	shown	montrer
shut	shut	shut	fermer
sing	sang	sung	chanter
sink	sank	sunk	sombrer
sit	sat	sat	être assis
sleep	slept	slept	dormir
smell	smelt	smelt	sentir (odorat)
speak	spoke	spoken	parler
spend	spent	spent	dépenser/passer du temps
spoil	spoilt	spoilt	gâcher, abîmer
spread	spread	spread	(se) répandre, étaler
stand	stood	stood	être debout
steal	stole	stolen	voler (dérober)
stick	stuck	stuck	coller
strike	struck	struck	frapper
sweep	swept	swept	balayer
swim	swam	swum	nager
take	took	taken	prendre
teach	taught	taught	enseigner
tear	tore	torn	déchirer
tell	told	told	dire, raconter
think	thought	thought	penser
throw	threw	thrown	jeter, lancer
understand	understood	understood	comprendre
wake up	woke up	woken up	se réveiller
wear	wore	worn	porter
win	won	won	gagner
write	wrote	written	écrire

Constructions prépositionnelles

Verbes

about → *worry about:* s'inquiéter de
after → *look after:* s'occuper de
at → *laugh at:* se moquer de
look at: regarder
back → *date back to:* remonter à (temps)
for → *apologise for:* s'excuser de
apply for: postuler à (une offre d'emploi)
blame somebody for something: reprocher quelque chose à quelqu'un
care for sth: aimer quelque chose
hope for: espérer
long for: désirer vivement
look for: chercher
sit for (*an exam*): se présenter à
wait for: attendre
from → *borrow sth from somebody:* emprunter quelque chose à quelqu'un
hear from somebody: avoir des nouvelles de quelqu'un
prevent somebody from doing something: empêcher quelqu'un de faire quelque chose
steal sth from somebody: voler quelque chose à quelqu'un
in → *participate in something:* participer à
into → *break into:* cambrioler
like → *feel like:* avoir envie de
look like: ressembler à
sound like: ressembler à (son)
taste like: ressembler à (goût)
of → *accuse of:* accuser de
approve of: approuver
complain of/about: se plaindre de
dream of: rêver de
(be) fond of: aimer, apprécier
hear of: entendre parler de
remind somebody of something: rappeler quelque chose à quelqu'un
take care of: s'occuper de
think of/about: penser à
on → *comment on:* commenter
depend on: dépendre de
get on/off: monter/descendre (d'un bus/train)
to → *belong to:* appartenir à
listen to: écouter
look forward to: attendre impatiemment
with → *agree with:* être d'accord avec
deal with: traiter (un sujet)

Adjectifs

about → *crazy about:* fou de
at → *angry at:* fâché à propos de
good at: bon en
surprised at: surpris de
for → *responsible for:* responsable de
sorry for: désolé de
from → *different from:* différent de
in → *interested in:* intéressé par
of → *aware of:* conscient de
capable of: capable de
proud of: fier de
tired of: fatigué de
on → *keen on:* passionné de
to → *contrary to:* contraire à
eager to: désireux de
kind to: aimable envers/avec
similar to: semblable à
with → *angry with:* fâché contre quelqu'un
busy with: occupé à
disappointed with: déçu de
pleased with: content de

Attention
Les verbes suivants se construisent sans préposition (contrairement au français) :
- ***answer:*** répondre à
- ***obey:*** obéir à
- ***remember:*** se souvenir de

Lexique

La traduction indiquée correspond au sens des mots rencontrés dans les exercices.

A

a few: quelques
above: au-dessus de
absent-minded: distrait
ache: faire mal
across: idée de « traverser », de l'autre côté de
again: encore, de nouveau
against: contre
agree with: être d'accord avec
ahead: devant
airsick (be): avoir le mal de l'air
alive: vivant
allow: autoriser
almost: presque
alone: seul
already: déjà
always: toujours
another: un autre
any: du, de la, des (négatif, interrogatif)
anybody: n'importe qui
anything: quelque chose (négatif, interrogatif)
apple: pomme
apply for (a job): postuler à (une offre d'emploi)
appoint: nommer, désigner
area: étendue
argue: se disputer, discuter
arm: bras
ashamed (be): avoir honte
ask for something: demander quelque chose
asleep: endormi
attend: assister à
attractive: attirant
awfully: terriblement

B

background: arrière-plan
bag: sac
balcony: balcon
bank holiday: jour férié
bat: chauve-souris
bathroom: salle de bains
be (v.i.)**:** être
be allowed to: avoir la permission de
be born: naître
be seasick: avoir le mal de mer
be wrong: avoir tort
be... left: rester
beach: plage
bear (n.)**:** ours
bear (v. i.)**:** supporter
beat (v. i.)**:** battre
become (v. i.)**:** devenir
beef: bœuf (viande)
beer: bière
belfry: beffoi
before: avant
beggar: mendiant
begin (v. i.)**:** commencer
beginning: début
behind: derrière
believe: croire
belong to: appartenir à
bell: cloche
bench: banc
bet (v. i.)**:** parier
better: meilleur, mieux
between: entre
big: grand, important
bike: vélo
bill: note, addition
bin: poubelle
bird: oiseau
birth: naissance
bite (v. i.)**:** mordre
bitter: amer
blackbird: merle
bless you!: à vos souhaits !
block: pâté de maisons
blood: sang
blow (v. i.)**:** souffler
boat: bateau
body: corps
boiled: bouilli
boring: ennuyeux
borrow something from someone: emprunter quelque chose à quelqu'un
boss: patron
brake: freiner
bread: pain
break (v. i.)**:** casser
break down (v. i.)**:** tomber en panne/ faire une dépression
breathe: respirer
breed: élever (un animal)
bright: brillant
bring (v. i.)**:** apporter, amener
bring up (v. i.)**:** élever (un enfant)
broad: large
brother: frère
brush: brosse, pinceau
buffalo: bison
build (v. i.)**:** bâtir
bump: heurter
burn (v. i.)**:** brûler
burst (v. i.)**:** éclater
butcher: boucher
butterfly: papillon
buy (v. i.)**:** acheter

C

cake: gâteau
calf: veau (animal)
call: appel
camera: appareil photo
cancel: annuler
car: voiture
car driver: automobiliste
careless: imprudent
case: cas, valise
cash: en espèces
cash desk: caisse
cashier: caissier
castle: château
catch (v. i.)**:** attraper
cattle: bétail
cauliflower: chou-fleur
century: siècle
change: monnaie
chat: bavarder
cheap: bon marché
check: vérifier
check in: enregistrer (des bagages)
cheeky: insolent
cheers!: à votre santé !
cheese: fromage
cherry: cerise
chicken: poulet
chilly: frisquet
chip: frite
choose (v. i.)**:** choisir
chop: côtelette
church: église
clap of thunder: coup de tonnerre
clean: nettoyer
clerk: employé
clever: astucieux
climb: grimper
cloud: nuage
coach: entraîneur
coal: charbon
coin: pièce de monnaie
cold: rhume, froid
come (v. i.)**:** venir
come back: revenir
come near: approcher
complete: terminer, achever
congratulate: féliciter
convenient: pratique
cook: cuisinier
cost (v. i.)**:** coûter
cosy: confortable
counter: comptoir, guichet
country: campagne, pays
cow: vache
crash: s'écraser
crazy: fou
cross: fâché, inamical
cross over: traverser
crossing: traversée
crossroads: croisement
crowd: foule

crowded: bondé
crown: couronne
currency: monnaie (nationale)
custard: crème anglaise
customs: douane
customs officer: douanier
cut (v. i.)**:** couper

D

day: jour
day off: jour de congé
daydream: rêvasser
death: mort
demonstration: manifestation
department store: grand magasin
depend on: dépendre de
desk: bureau (meuble)
dial: composer un numéro de téléphone
die: mourir
dirty: sale
disagree with: ne pas être d'accord avec
disappointed: déçu
disease: maladie
dish: plat
district: quartier
do (v. i.)**:** faire
dog: chien
draw (v. i.)**:** tirer, dessiner
drawer: tiroir
dream of: rêver de
dress: robe
drink (n.)**:** boisson
drink (v. i.)**:** boire
drive (v. i.)**:** conduire (une voiture)
drive in (v. i.)**:** enfoncer
drive past (v. i.)**:** passer devant (en voiture)
driver: conducteur
driving licence: permis de conduire
dry: sec
dumb: muet
during: pendant

E

each: chaque
ear: oreille
early: de bonne heure, tôt, en avance
earring: boucle d'oreille
Easter: Pâques
easy: facile
eat (v. i.)**:** manger
either... or: ou... ou
elect: élire
end: fin, bout
end: finir
engagement: fiançailles
engineer: ingénieur
enjoy: prendre plaisir à, aimer
enough: assez (de)
every: tous les, chaque
everybody: tout le monde
exciting: passionnant
executive: cadre (entreprise)
expect: (s')attendre (à)
expensive: cher
eye: œil

F

face: visage
face: affronter
factory: usine
fair: blond
fall (v. i.)**:** tomber
fast: rapide
fasten: attacher
fat: gros, gras
feather: plume (oiseau)
fed up with (be) : en avoir assez de
feed (v. i.)**:** nourrir
feel (v. i.)**:** (se) sentir
feel like: avoir envie de
fellow: camarade, collègue
few (a): quelques
fight (v. i.)**:** se battre
find (v. i.)**:** trouver
fine: beau
fire: licencier
fit: en forme
fit: aller (vêtement)
flash of lightning: éclair
flat: appartement
flavour: assaisonner, parfumer
flight: vol (air)
flower: fleur
flu: grippe
fly (v. i.)**:** voler (air)
fly: mouche
fond of (be): apprécier, aimer
food: nourriture
for: pendant, depuis
foreground: premier plan
forget (v. i.)**:** oublier
forgive (v. i.)**:** pardonner
forward: en avant
fox: renard
free: libre
freeze (v. i.)**:** geler
French beans: haricots verts
fried potatoes: frites
friend: ami
friendly: amical
frightened: effrayé
frog: grenouille
from: de (provenance)
fuel: carburant
full-time: à plein temps
fun (have): s'amuser
funfair: foire
funny: drôle
fur: fourrure
furniture: meubles
fussy: méticuleux

G

garden: jardin
gate: grille d'entrée, portail
get (v. i.)**:** obtenir
get off (v. i.)**:** descendre de (bus, avion...)
get on (v. i.)**:** monter dans (bus, train)
get on well (v. i.)**:** bien s'entendre
get out (v. i.)**:** sortir
get up (v. i.)**:** monter, se lever
give (v. i.)**:** donner
glad: content
glass: verre
go (v. i.)**:** aller
go on (v. i.)**:** continuer
go sightseeing (v. i.)**:** faire du tourisme
go wrong (v. i.)**:** aller de travers
goal: but marqué (football)
goalkeeper: gardien de but
good at: bon en
grapefruit: pamplemousse
grass: herbe
Greek: grec
green: vert
grey: gris
grow (v. i.)**:** pousser, faire pousser (plantes)
guilty: coupable
guinea-pig: cobaye, cochon d'Inde

H

hair: cheveux
ham: jambon
hammer: marteau
hand: main
handbag: sac à main
handkerchief: mouchoir
hang (v. i.)**:** pendre, suspendre
happen: arriver, se produire
happiness: bonheur
happy: heureux
hard: dur
hard-boiled: dur (œuf)
hare: lièvre
have (v. i.)**:** avoir
have a rest: se reposer
have fun: s'amuser
head: tête
headache: migraine
headmaster: proviseur, directeur
health: santé
hear (v. i.)**:** entendre
hear from someone (v. i.)**:** recevoir des nouvelles de quelqu'un
hear of (v. i.)**:** entendre parler de
heartily: chaleureusement
heavy: lourd
help: aider
helpful: serviable
hide (v. i.)**:** (se) cacher
hill: colline
hire: embaucher
hit (v. i.)**:** frapper
hold (v. i.)**:** tenir
hope: espérer
horse: cheval
hot: chaud
how long: combien de temps

how many: combien (pluriel)
how much: combien (singulier)
hug: prendre dans ses bras
hungry (be): avoir faim
hurry (be in a): être pressé
hurt (v. i.)**:** faire mal

I

ice: glace
icy: glacial
if: si (condition)
ill: malade
in front of: devant
included: inclus, compris
income tax: impôt sur le revenu
incredible: incroyable
information: renseignements
inside: à l'intérieur (de)
instead of: au lieu de
insurance: assurance (voiture)
interested in (be) : s'intéresser à
iron: fer
island: île

J

joke: plaisanter
journey: voyage
juice: jus (fruit)

K

keep (v. i.)**:** garder
key: clé
kill: tuer
kind: gentil, aimable
kindness: gentillesse
kitchen: cuisine
knock: frapper
knock down: abattre
know (v. i.)**:** savoir, connaître

L

ladder: échelle
lake: lac
lamb: agneau
lamp-post: réverbère
land: atterrir, débarquer
last: dernier
last: durer
late: en retard
laugh at: rire
laugh: se moquer de
law: loi
lawn: pelouse
lawnmower: tondeuse à gazon
lazy: paresseux
lead (v. i.)**:** mener
leaf: feuille (arbre)
learn (v. i.)**:** apprendre
leave (v. i.)**:** laisser, partir
left (be): rester
leg: jambe, pied de table
lemon: citron
lend (v. i.)**:** prêter
let (v. i.)**:** laisser, autoriser
liar: menteur
lie: mentir
life: vie
lift: ascenseur
light: clair
like: aimer
like (be): ressembler à
limb: membre (corps)
listen to: écouter
little (a): un peu (de)
live: vivre, habiter
lock: serrure
look: regard
look: sembler, paraître
look after: s'occuper de
look at: regarder
look for: chercher
look up: chercher (dictionnaire)
lose (v. i.)**:** perdre
lot (a ... of): beaucoup de (pluriel)
loud: fort (son, voix)
luck: chance
luggage: bagages

M

mad: fou
make (v. i.)**:** faire
makeup: maquillage
make up one's mind (v. i.)**:** se décider
manage: se débrouiller
manager: directeur
many: beaucoup de (pluriel)
map: carte (géographie)
mark: note (examen)
match: s'accorder avec
mate: camarade
matter: être important
mayor: maire
meal: repas
mean (v. i.)**:** vouloir dire, signifier
meaning: sens, signification
means: moyen
meat: viande
mechanic: mécanicien
medicine: médicament
meet (v. i.)**:** rencontrer
midday: midi
middle: milieu
milk: lait
mind: être égal, gêner
mind!: attention!
misty: brumeux
monkey: singe
mountain: montagne
mouse: souris
mouth: bouche
mow (v. i.)**:** tondre (pelouse)
much: beaucoup de (singulier)
murderer: assassin
mushroom: champignon
must: devoir
mutton: mouton (viande)

N

nail: clou
nasty: mauvais, méchant
near: près de
need: avoir besoin de
neighbour: voisin, prochain
neither: non plus
never: jamais
new: nouveau
news: nouvelles
next: prochain
nobody: personne
noise: bruit
noisy: bruyant
not... yet: pas encore
notice: remarquer
novel: roman
nowadays: de nos jours
numerous: nombreux
nurse: infirmier

O

office: bureau (pièce)
often: souvent
only: seulement
open (in the): en plein air
order: commander
other: autre
outside: dehors, hors de
over: terminé
own: posséder
ox: bœuf (animal)

P

pack up: faire ses bagages
painful: douloureux
paint: peindre
painting: peinture
palace: palais
pan: casserole
paper: papier, journal
parcel: paquet
pardon me?: pardon ?
park: (se) garer
park: square
parrot: perroquet
part-time: à temps partiel
pass: réussir (examen)
passenger: passager, voyageur
pavement: trottoir
pay for something (v. i.)**:** payer quelque chose
peas: petits pois
pedestrian: piéton
pedestrian crossing: passage piéton
people: gens
perfume: parfum
petrol station: station-service
phone: téléphoner
pick up: ramasser, prendre quelqu'un (voiture)
piece: morceau

pig: cochon
pill: pilule
place: lieu, endroit
plane: avion
plate: assiette
pleasant: agréable
please: faire plaisir à
pleased: content
pleasure: plaisir
pork: porc (viande)
postcard: carte postale
poster: affiche
potato: pomme de terre
pour: pleuvoir à verse
powerful: puissant
prescription: ordonnance
present: actuel
pretty: joli
properly: correctement
purse: porte-monnaie
put (v. i.)**:** mettre
put on (v. i.)**:** mettre (vêtement)
put off (v. i.)**:** éteindre (lumière)

Q

quarrel: se disputer
queen: reine
queue up: faire la queue
quite: tout à fait

R

rabbit: lapin
race: course
race driver: pilote de course
railings: grillage, grilles
rain: pleuvoir
rainy: pluvieux
rather: plutôt
read (v. i.)**:** lire
ready: prêt
receptionist: réceptionniste
red: rouge
referee: arbitre
regularly: régulièrement
remember: se rappeler
remind someone of something: rappeler quelque chose à quelqu'un
rent (v. i.)**:** louer
research: recherche
responsible for: responsable de
rest: repos
rest: se reposer
return ticket: billet aller-retour
returns (many happy): bon anniversaire
ride (v. i.)**:** aller à bicyclette
right (be): avoir raison
right: droit
right now: immédiatement
ring (v. i.)**:** sonner
rise (v. i.)**:** s'élever
roof: toit
room: espace, pièce
rude: mal élevé, grossier
run (v. i.)**:** courir
run over: écraser

S

sail: naviguer
sailor: marin
salesman/woman: vendeur/vendeuse
same: même
save: sauver
say (v. i.)**:** dire
scared: effrayé
scientist: scientifique
score: marquer (un but)
scoreboard: tableau d'affichage (sport)
sea: mer
seasick (be): avoir le mal de mer
seat: place, siège
second-hand (adj.): d'occasion
see (v. i.)**:** voir
seem: sembler
sell (v. i.)**:** vendre
send (v. i.)**:** envoyer
set (v. i.)**:** poser, placer
several: plusieurs
shake (v. i.)**:** secouer
share: partager
sheep: mouton(s) (animal)
shine (v. i.)**:** briller
ship: navire
shoe: chaussure
shoot (v. i.)**:** tirer (arme à feu)
shop: magasin
shop assistant: vendeur
shop window: vitrine
shore: rivage
short of: à court de
shoulder: épaule
shout: crier
show (v. i.)**:** montrer
shut (v. i.)**:** fermer
shy: timide
sick: malade
sightseeing: voir *go sightseeing*
sign: enseigne
silly: idiot
silver: argent (métal)
since: depuis
sing (v. i.)**:** chanter
singer: chanteur
single ticket: aller simple
sink: évier
sink (v. i.)**:** sombrer
sister: sœur
sit (v. i.)**:** être assis
sitting room: salon
skin: peau
sky: ciel
slap: gifler
sleep (v. i.)**:** dormir
small: petit
smell (v. i.)**:** sentir (odorat)
smile: sourire
smoke: fumer
snake: serpent
snatch: arracher
sneakers: chaussures de tennis
snow: neiger
so: aussi, si (exclamatif)
soap: savon
soccer player (n.)**:** joueur de football
some: du, de la, des (positif)
sometimes: parfois
soon (as ... as): aussitôt que
sound like: ressembler à (son)
speak (v. i.)**:** parler
speech: discours
speed: vitesse
spend (v. i.)**:** passer (temps, vacances), dépenser
spider: araignée
spit (v. i.)**:** cracher
spoil (v. i.)**:** gâcher, abîmer
spread (v. i.)**:** (se) répandre, étaler
square: place (ville)
staff: personnel
staircase: escalier
stand (v. i.)**:** se tenir debout, supporter (qqun, qqch)
stand up (v. i.)**:** se lever, se mettre debout
start: démarrer
state: état
stay: rester
steal (v. i.)**:** voler (dérober)
step: marche (escalier), pas
stick (v. i.)**:** coller
still: encore
stir: remuer
storm: orage, tempête
stormy: orageux
story: histoire
strawberry: fraise
street: rue
strike (v. i.)**:** frapper, sonner
student: élève
study: étude
study: étudier
stuff: truc, machin (fam.)
subway: métro
succeed: réussir
such: tel
such, such a: si (exclamatif)
suitcase: valise
sun: soleil
support: soutenir, encourager
surround: entourer
swallow: avaler
sweat: sueur
sweep (v. i.)**:** balayer
sweet: sucré
sweet: dessert, bonbon
swim (v. i.)**:** nager
swimming-pool: piscine
switch off: éteindre (lumière, TV)
switch on: allumer (lumière, TV)

T

take (v. i.)**:** prendre
take a walk: se promener
take care of: s'occuper de

take off (v. i.)**:** décoller (avion), ôter (vêtement)
talk: bavarder
tall: grand (taille)
tap: robinet
taste like: avoir le goût de
teach (v. i.)**:** enseigner
team: équipe
tear: larme
tear (v. i.)**:** déchirer
teenager: adolescent
tell (v. i.)**:** dire, raconter
temper: caractère, humeur
temperature: fièvre
terrific: super
that: qui, que (relatif)
then: puis, alors
there is/are: il y a
thick: épais
thin: mince
think of, about (v. i.)**:** penser à
thriller: film, roman à suspense
throw (v. i.)**:** jeter, lancer
tie: cravate
tight: étroit
time: fois
tip: pourboire
tired: fatigué
tiring: fatigant
today: aujourd'hui
too: trop
top: sommet
towel: serviette de toilette
town: ville
town hall: mairie
trade: métier
traffic: circulation (automobile)
traffic jam: embouteillage
traffic lights: feux tricolores
traffic warden: agent de la circulation
train: (s')entraîner
traitor: traître
travel: voyager
travelling: voyager (le fait de…)
treasure: trésor
tree: arbre
trouble (in): en difficulté
true: vrai
truth: vérité
try: essayer
try on: essayer (vêtement)
tube: métro
turkey: dinde
turn off: éteindre (lumière, TV)
turn on: allumer (lumière, TV)
TV set: poste de télévision
twice: deux fois
type: taper à la machine

U

under: sous
understand (v. i.)**:** comprendre
unemployed: au chômage
unfortunately: malheureusement
up to now: jusqu'à maintenant
use: utiliser
useful: utile
useless: inutile
usually: habituellement

V

van: camionnette
veal: veau (viande)
vegetable: légume
versus ou vs.: contre (sport)
voice: voix

W

wait for: attendre
waiter: garçon de café
wake up (v. i.)**:** (se) réveiller
walk: marcher
wallet: portefeuille
want: vouloir
war: guerre
wash: (se) laver
washbasin: lavabo
watch: montre
watch: assister
water: eau
wave: vague
way: chemin
weak: faible
wear: porter (vêtement)
weather: temps (météo)
wedding: mariage
week: semaine
welcome: accueillir
welcome (you are): de rien
wet: mouillé, humide
whale: baleine
what, what a: quel, quelle, quels, quelles (exclamatif)
what… for: à quoi, pour quoi
what… like: à quoi (ressemblance)
wheel: roue
where: où
which: quel, quelle, quels, quelles, (interrogatif) ; qui, que (relatif)
while: pendant que
white: blanc
white coffee: café au lait
who: qui
whose: dont
wife: épouse
win (v. i.)**:** gagner (sport, jeu)
wind: vent
window: fenêtre
wine: vin
wing: aile
wish: souhaiter
without: sans
wolf: loup
wonder: se demander
wood: bois
wool: laine
work: travailler, fonctionner
worker: travailleur, ouvrier
world: monde
worried: inquiet
worry: s'inquiéter
wrap up: envelopper
write (v. i.)**:** écrire

Y

year: année
yellow: jaune
yesterday: hier
young: jeune

Vocabulaire : bilan sous forme de jeux

1 *The longest snake*

Pour faire un serpent de mots, sélectionnez plusieurs mots dans le lexique (pages 54-58) et écrivez-les les uns à la suite des autres. Chaque mot se termine par une lettre (bien sûr !) et le mot suivant doit commencer par cette même lettre. Continuez ce serpent aussi longtemps que vous le pourrez.

Snake – ear – rain ....

....

2 *Words in a word*

Dans un mot peuvent se cacher plusieurs mots.
Ex. : dans « *beat* », on peut trouver *a, at, be, tea, bat*.
Trouvez autant de mots que possible dans les adjectifs suivants (attention ! tous les mots doivent se trouver dans le lexique page 54–58).

1. EMBARRASSED

....

....

2. ENTHUSIASTIC

....

....

3 Proverbes et expressions

En français comme en anglais, on utilise souvent des expressions basées sur des noms d'animaux, mais ce ne sont pas toujours les mêmes ! D'après le sens, associez les expressions françaises à leurs équivalents anglais. Attention ! Parfois, les noms d'animaux ne se trouvent que dans une seule des deux langues.

1. Avoir un chat dans la gorge. •	• a. As free as a bird.
2. Quand le chat n'est pas là, les souris dansent. •	• b. The early bird catches the worm.
3. Vendre la mèche. •	• c. I have other fish to fry.
4. J'ai d'autres chats à fouetter. •	• d. I wish I were a fly on the wall.
5. Muet comme une carpe. •	• e. To have a frog in one's throat.
6. Avoir une araignée au plafond. •	• f. To let the cat out of the bag.
7. La fortune appartient à ceux qui se lèvent tôt. •	• g. As happy as a lark.
8. Myope comme une taupe. •	• h. As blind as a bat.
9. Malin comme un singe. •	• i. As dumb as a fish.
10. Libre comme l'air. •	• j. When pigs can fly.
11. Il pleut des cordes. •	• k. When the cat's away, the mice will play.
12. J'aimerais être une petite souris. •	• l. To have a bat in the belfry.
13. Quand les poules auront des dents. •	• m. As sly as a fox.
14. Gai comme un pinson. •	• n. It's raining cats and dogs.

Pour faire cet exercice *"you have to keep cool"* ! Les Anglais diraient : *"you have to keep cool as a cucumber!"*

4 *Crossword*

Les définitions sont en français ; les mots à trouver sont en anglais.

Across

1. Veille du dimanche.
2. Résultat sportif.
3. Exprime une condition.
4. Début d'éléphant. – Pas lourd.
5. Chiffre.
6. Se prennent à 17 heures, en Angleterre.
7. Forme de *be*. – Brise le silence.
9. Dans un jardin ou une forêt. – Lundi, par exemple.

Down

A. Personne qui étudie la science.
B. Elles volent dans les airs.
C. Article à l'envers.
D. Ce n'est pas utile.
E. Deux consonnes du mot *race*.
F. Auxiliaire. – Pas du tout en l'air.
G. Après tout, c'est une arche anglaise.
H. Aujourd'hui, c'est déjà du passé.

PEFC
10-31-2065
Certifié PEFC
pefc-france.org

Achevé d'imprimer en décembre 2018 par Pollina en France - 26824
N° éditeur : 2018_0311 - Dépôt légal : Décembre 2018